BRONC BUSTER

Doc Beck Westerns Book 6

SARAH ELISABETH SAWYER

PROLOGUE

"I'm telling you, they're eating our sheep," Willie whispered, her voice squeaky.

Not a breeze stirred the lodgepole pines that rose to the heavens around Wayne, his sister Willie, and brother Roy as they crouched on the edge of the cliff. The siblings were scrunched in a pocket of snow-covered rocks and pines, a place they called the hand of God. From up there, they could see anything worth seeing in the Medicine Bow Mountains.

If they turned around, there was one of the best grass meadows to graze their uncle's sheep herd. But right where they were facing, in a valley, was a campsite being used by parties unknown.

Wayne only knew that whoever those men were, they didn't belong there, which meant they were up to no good. Just like his sister, Willie, said. Those men were eating their sheep.

That was plain enough by a clump of dirty wool and leftover carcass laying at the edge of the empty camp. Smoke wisped from the died-out campfire, skimming over the single canvas tent and vanishing into the pines. Whoever these men were, they planned to stick around awhile and keep eating the siblings' sheep.

Wayne was belly-up on one of the boulders where he had crawled up to get a better look, careful to not put a hand in the snow. It wasn't really cold because of the early summer sunshine, but it was wet. He used his palms to push himself backwards, sliding to the ground.

Roy covered his hatless head with one arm to protect himself from the pebbles that Wayne accidentally kicked. Roy's other arm was securely fastened around their collie's neck, holding her close as he trembled.

Wayne squatted beside his younger brother—who wasn't really his younger brother since the three of them were triplets—and patted his arm. "Sorry about that, Willie-Roy."

Willie squatted beside Roy, grabbing her worn hat with both hands. She pulled the brim over her ears, blue eyes bright and wide. "What are we gonna do? Uncle Rufus will skin us alive for losing sheep."

"Don't reckon we can get that one back," Wayne said. "But whoever them fellas are, they're up to something. Ain't no good hunting this side of the mountain, no gold prospecting. I reckon they're hiding out from the law or something."

Roy shook harder. Valor, their dog, licked his chin while Willie patted his arm. "It's okay, Roy. We won't let nothing happen to you."

Wayne plopped his own hat over Roy's blonde hair that matched his own, and helped his brother up. "We got to tell Uncle Rufus. He'll know what to do."

Willie's eyebrows shot up. "He will?"

Wayne couldn't say anything other than, "Sure he will."

The triplets skittered down the path leading them off the cliff, then through the woods. They had sheltered the sheep in Leg Bend Canyon with rough cedar rails to hold them in. That wouldn't keep coyotes or wolves out, but it was two-legged wolves that Wayne was worried about.

Roy used Valor as a crutch while he tried to keep up with the loping pace of his siblings. They ran as fast as they could over the uneven terrain, tripping over exposed roots and rock in their oversized boots. Wayne had a big hole in his left boot where his big toe would've poked through if his foot was full grown. And even though it was too warm for their cast-off men's jackets, wearing them was easier than carrying them and better than being without them at night.

The triplets stumbled headlong into the briar patch yard in front of the cabin. It was no worse than the shanty in Drybone, where they lived when they weren't grazing sheep in the green meadows of the mountains.

The siblings leaped onto the porch, heavy boots thumping on the rotten boards. Willie's foot went through one of the boards, but she quickly caught herself on the side of the wall.

Wayne pushed the sagging door of the cabin open, calling as he went, "Uncle Rufus! There are men camped out near the meadow and they—"

All the racket must have scared Uncle Rufus bad. He was laying across the cot in the back corner and didn't wake gentle. He charged up right in the bed, lurking forward, pistol in hand. It went off, shooting a hole clean through the broken front window.

Willie pushed Roy down behind the empty flour bin. Valor barked mightily.

Wayne ducked, using both arms to cover his head. "Uncle Rufus, it's us!"

Uncle Rufus staggered into one wall, hitting his shoulder hard and dropping the pistol. He rubbed his eyes with both fists and blinked as he looked around the room.

There wasn't much to see—the fireplace and hearth that was missing several stones. Empty crates and a whiskey barrel served as chairs at the wobbly table.

Uncle Rufus kicked two empty whiskey bottles, sending them spinning across the floor as he stepped toward Wayne.

"What do you think you're doing, Willie-Wayne, barging in on me in the middle of the night!" He shook a finger in Wayne's face. "I've shot men for less than that."

Wayne grimaced. "Uncle Rufus, it's the middle of the day."

Rufus blinked, dropping his hand and looking around the sun-filled cabin. Willie peeked out from behind the flour bin, her long, mousy blonde-brown hair falling over her shoulder. Willie's longer hair was about the only way people could tell her and her dirty-faced brothers apart. Roy stayed tucked behind the flour bin.

Taking in a deep breath and a swallow of courage, Wayne tried again. "Uncle Rufus, there's some men camped out by the meadow. They got one of the sheep and they've been eating on it."

Uncle Rufus turned in a staggering circle, looking the walls up and down as if they had answers. He came to a stop facing Wayne again, staring over his head that barely reach the height of Rufus's chest. At 10 years old, Wayne couldn't wait to be as tall as his uncle.

Rufus kept staring over his head, blinking against the glaring light coming through the open door. Then he grabbed Wayne by the lapels of the old jacket and shook him so hard his teeth rattled.

"You let someone steal my sheep? You three worthless, good for nothing kids. And now you've gone and left the whole flock to come crying to me!"

Above the ringing in his ears, Wayne heard a growl before Uncle Rufus yelped and let Wayne go.

Wayne fell on his backside, eyes swirling. But he could see Roy wrapped around Uncle Rufus' legs while their dog wrestled the man, her mouth clamped onto one arm. Uncle Rufus' free arm windmilled. He lost his balance and fell backwards.

Willie had come from behind the flour bin at the same time as Roy. Her hands were tucked under Wayne's armpits, trying to lift him from behind with all her little might. Wayne helped by pushing with his feet and soon, he was standing.

Still dizzy, he let Willie pull him through the open door as he shouted behind him, "Come on, Willie-Roy!"

His little brother untangled himself from the irate Rufus, who fought himself trying to get up.

Roy ran out the door and grabbed Wayne around the waist, holding tight, tears rolling down his cheeks and over his always silent mouth.

Wayne sucked in a breath and gave a shrill whistle. Their courageous dog released Rufus' arm and bounded out the door.

Together, they stumbled down the stump steps, a string of cursing following them across the briar patch yard and back to the wildness of the Medicine Bow Mountains.

CHAPTER 1

Eyes squeezed shut, Jimmy's seat slammed in the saddle. He clenched the reins and the filly's mane as he went airborne again, knees tight to stay onboard. He locked his jaw to keep his teeth from clinking together as he descended once again.

Bam!

Up, then bam!

Again, and again. But Jimmy could feel the filly's rhythm slowing. He adjusted his seat, settling in and loosening his knees as his free hand found the saddle horn for the final crow hops the filly offered.

Eyes still closed, Jimmy could feel the ripple of the filly's muscles beneath him, her shoulders rolling as she took a tentative step forward. Her body trembled beneath his legs, the tremble of fatigue of one who had fought what was right long enough. She was surrendering.

Applause sounded. Jimmy opened his eyes to find an audience had gathered around the corral where the McKinnon ranch hands were busting broncs all day.

This was his third to gentle and for some reason, other hands gradually stopped what they were doing and gathered around the corral to watch. Even Stubby Goodman, the bunkhouse cook, was standing at the corner of the barn, sharpening a knife with spit and boot leather. The salt and pepper mustache over his lips twitched. A smile?

Jimmy gently turned the filly in a circle, observing how she kept her head level, ears swiveling as he spoke softly to her, stroking her neck with his gloved hand. "That's a girl. You're doing just fine."

"So are you," a female voice said.

Jimmy's hands jerked, causing the filly to side-dance. Had the filly really answered?

But when Jimmy glanced around, he realized a girl was standing on the bottom rail of the corral. She wore a long-sleeved pink calico dress, her slender arms wrapped around a post as she lounged to one side, grinning at him.

It was Daphne Peele, daughter of Mr. Brendan Peele, a neighboring rancher who was visiting today. Mr. Peele was up at the main house now, talking to Doc McKinnon about selling him more horses. Jimmy hadn't known Daphne Peele had come along, nor that she had made her way down to the corrals.

While the other ranch hands got the next bronc ready for busting, Jimmy swung down from the horse, his cheeks burning hot. He fumbled with the cinch, but one of the other hands was already leading the filly away, leaving nothing between Jimmy and the fence...and Daphne Peele.

She giggled. "I hear tell you're the best bronc buster on this ranch. Maybe in the whole state of Wyoming."

Jimmy shoved his hands in his jacket pockets, his chin tucked as he stared at the hard packed dirt.

"I don't reckon that's entirely true, ma'am. The Good Lord is just always looking out for me."

Steve Bowers, head wrangler of the McKinnon Ranch, ambled over and climbed to the top rail beside Daphne. He swung his leg over it like he was mounting a horse, and slouched forward to rest one arm across his knee.

"Aw now, Miss Daphne, Jimmy's being modest. He's not only a great bronc buster, he also takes care of the chickens. Speaking of which, Jimmy boy, ain't it time for you to collect eggs? Don't forget to leave those hatching ones alone."

There were chuckles from the ranch hands still hanging around the corral, nothing to do until the next horse was saddled. Stubby snorted and headed back for his kitchen on the other side of the bunkhouse.

Jimmy looked up at Steve, grinning. "Sure, Steve, I'll get right on that."

Since he'd been made head wrangler on the McKinnon Ranch last month, Jimmy hadn't noticed much change in Steve. He was still a happy-go-lucky fellow that gave and took his share of teasing.

What was more, Steve showed a lot of respect for Doc McKinnon, Laramie Jones, and most especially Miss Rebekah. That made him the kind of friend Jimmy wanted to have.

Jimmy vaulted over the fence and heard a girlish coo behind him.

"Is there anything that boy can't do?"

Jimmy quickened his steps, face flaming hot. The only females he ever cared to be around were Miss Rebekah. And his horse Kate.

CHAPTER 2

An intense discussion was underway in Doctor McKinnon's study. Rebekah sensed it before she stepped through the doorway. One look at Doctor McKinnon's face where he sat behind his desk, scratching out notes, told her he was worried.

Laramie Jones sat in one of the burgundy leather wingback chairs positioned before the desk. Mr. Brendon Peele, distinguished by his salt and pepper walrus mustache, occupied the other.

Laramie noticed Rebekah first and stood, his Stetson dangling loose in one hand. Mr. Peele and Doctor McKinnon followed suit as Rebekah stepped further inside.

"I didn't mean to interrupt. Freddy sent me to tell you lunch will be ready shortly."

Laramie perched on the corner of the desk, while Doctor McKinnon sighed and reseated himself, along with Mr. Peele.

"It's all right, Becka," Doctor McKinnon said. "Brendon came to let me know he only has ten head of horses he can sell me for filling that contract."

Rebekah rested her hands on top of the empty wingback chair. "You're still short?"

Doctor McKinnon rubbed his forehead as he leaned back in his swivel chair. "I'm afraid so. We still need twenty additional head to make the contract. I'd ask for an extension, but Glenn Butler had already requested two. Seems he far over bid this contract, and even with the horses I obtained from him, it won't be enough."

Through the open window between the floor-to-ceiling bookcases, loud whooping drifted up from the corral.

Rebekah glanced out the window. "I know the boys have worked hard."

Laramie shifted off the desk and moved to the window. "They're earning their plate of beans today."

Rebekah joined him at the window. He turned, looking down to meet her eyes with his hazel ones, ones that changed colors like the seasons and landscapes of their lives. Like his name did in her mind now, from Laramie Jones to Lee Stafford.

There was a worried look in those eyes now. Something beyond the short number of horses bothered him.

Rebekah knew it wouldn't be a pleasant thing for Lee to take the herd to Fort McKinney and face the uniform he was dishonorably discharged in. But he'd done the right thing then, even though it cost him everything.

A few years after his promotion to captain, Lee disobeyed orders to rout a band of Omaha Indians who had gone on a summer hunt. It was a traditional trip her people had taken for generations, even on the reservation. Rebekah was born on the prairie in a teepee during one of those hunts.

But the summer of 1890 was different. The ghost dance had spread like a wildfire throughout Indian country. Thousands of Indians were seemingly in a frenzy with hope that the Creator would drive out the white people, bring back the buffalo, and return all Indians to their homelands.

Few Omahas were caught up in the prophecy of Wovoka, a Northern Paiute religious leader. None of them were a threat. Yet some in the U.S. Cavalry, after decades of clashes with Indians, regarded them all as savages.

Lee's orders to round up the hunting Omaha Indians by force would have almost surely led to a massacre like what took place that winter at Wounded Knee in South Dakota. Rebekah had gone there to help treat the survivors, and she saw firsthand what Lee prevented among her own people.

He saved lives that summer—including her own brother's, who was among the Omaha hunting party.

But now he had to face the pain of those memories, the disgrace and loss, when he took Doctor McKinnon's horses to Fort McKinney. His past would be revealed to the ranch hands, and subsequently scatter across Wyoming.

Not even Doctor McKinnon knew of Lee's past, of getting kicked out of the cavalry. He'd hired Lee solely on Rebekah's endorsement.

Rebekah threaded her hand through Lee's arm as she gave him a reassuring squeeze. "I will stand by you no matter what."

His voice dropped low and deep—for her ears only. "I like the sound of that mighty fine."

Something in his tone, something that came straight from his heart, caused Rebekah to lose her breath. Those warm colors in Lee's eyes were changing seasons again, tinged with a hope she couldn't fulfill.

She couldn't, and keep her pledge to serve her people on the reservation. Marriage, a family of her own—her life was too committed already.

She dropped her hand. Perhaps it was time to leave the ranch again, and soon. Very soon.

CHAPTER 3

Before Freddy called them to the noon meal, Brendon Peele asked to see the stock the ranch hands were working down in the corral. His request came in time to save Rebekah from fleeing the room on her own.

Down at the corral, a crowd had gathered by the five-rail timber fence. Rebekah noticed Daphne Peele had a seat on the top rail, her skirts blown by the wind nearly up to her knees. She was a bold young lady, and liked to hang around the boys whenever she could. And right then, despite Steve talking to her, she seemed to have her eye on one particular boy. Just Jimmy.

He was close to the barn, tightening leather strips that kept his gloves on while riding the broncs. Laramie Jones climbed the fence and helped prepare the next horse.

Doctor McKinnon motioned for Rebekah to join him at a spot beside the corral, Brendon Peele on his other side.

Doctor McKinnon nodded toward Jimmy. "I think they're letting him have his day. From what I've heard, Jimmy's gentled more horses than the other men combined."

While Rebekah knew the hands would gladly let the new man take bruises and broken bones in their place, she imagined it would be worth it to Jimmy. Even if he was immensely sore tonight.

A snort sounded from the other side of Daphne. Steve said, "Not quite, Doc. He'll only have done that if he breaks this one without it breaking him. "

Brendon Peale shook his head. "I hope this isn't all for nothing for your boys, Robert."

This got Steve's attention and he came over to stand with the two ranchers. He looked well put together for being the head wrangler, hardly any dirt on his smooth-shaven face. He was young enough to work long, hard hours, and keep good-looking while doing it.

"What do you mean? These are the last horses we need to fill the contract, ain't it, Doc McKinnon?"

Doctor McKinnon turned his attention back to the corral. Rebekah put her hand on his shoulder, wanting to absorb some of his distress. It wasn't good for a man's heart to be so worried, especially at his age. As a doctor, Robert McKinnon knew that, but this was Rebekah's way of reminding him.

He patted her hand to let her know he appreciated the thought. "I'm afraid not, Steve. We're still twenty horses short. I don't know where else I can rustle up more without having them shipped from South Dakota. But the cost would make all this not worth it."

In the center of the corral, Laramie and another hand held Jimmy's next target in place, a bay horse who pawed the ground. Jimmy approached the horse quietly, giving it a stroke on the neck. Everyone seemed captured by his calm yet purposeful movements.

Most everyone. Steve cleared his throat. "Doc, what about the herd in the Medicine Bow Mountains?"

Doctor McKinnon, not taking his eyes off the mesmerizing scene as Jimmy prepared to mount, murmured, "Hmm?"

Steve tried again. "There's a band of horses near Broke Leg

Canyon, left there by a failed rancher a few years ago. All I need to do—all *we* need to do—is cut out the number you need. We'll build temporary corrals to break them before bringing them down."

"I don't think there's time for that, Steve."

"There would be if we herded them right over the mountain and meet Laramie and the main herd on the other side in Drybone. I can do it, Doc McKinnon."

Jimmy checked the cinch and gently shortened the stirrups. Then he slowly put one foot in the stirrup, not letting the horse feel any pressure. In one swift motion, he nodded at Laramie and the other hand who released the horse's head as Jimmy sprang aboard.

The horse crow hopped before Jimmy was even seated, but he didn't come off. Jimmy threw one hand back for balance as the horse ducked its head and went into a bucking extravaganza.

Rebekah marveled as Jimmy held his seat, his eyes squeezed shut. She counted the number of times his vertebrae was being compressed with each slam in the saddle. But the ride was too impressive for her to worry too much. He was young and strong and finding his place, maybe even his forever home, there on the McKinnon Ranch.

With a mighty surge, the bay snapped the left rein and Daphne gasped. Jimmy still kept his eyes closed, his hand finding the saddle horn and he held on for several more bucks.

Finally, the horse settled enough for Jimmy to leap off in a single bound, the broken reins flopping loose. Rebekah joined in the applause for him while the other hand took the horse to cool him. Laramie clapped Jimmy on the shoulder, saying something that made Jimmy shrug with a grin.

Daphne let out a girlish squeal. "He's the best rider in the whole state of Wyoming!"

Steve cleared his throat loudly. "What do you think, Doc? About that herd? All right if we give it a try?"

Doctor McKinnon and Rebekah turned. She didn't miss the irritation in Steve's voice, and neither did the ranch owner.

Doctor McKinnon faced Steve square on, giving him his full attention. Steve looked like he wanted to shrink back, but held his own.

While Doctor McKinnon observed him, Rebekah did too, recalling when she first met the young greenhorn a few years ago.

She came upon him at a railroad station in Denver, Colorado. Some rowdy cowpokes were teaching Steve to dance by firing six-shooter rounds at his feet.

Rebekah stepped in to stop the nonsense. An ounce of prevention was worth a pound of cure. She'd patched up enough bullet holes in men's feet after such hazing.

After the cowpokes moved along, Rebekah started to as well, but Steve latched on to her and told her all about his dream of living in the west. Rebekah couldn't leave such a naïve boy of good character in the wild, knowing how quickly he would be ruined, if not consumed.

So, she rounded him and his gear up and took him on her next medical assignment before herding him to the McKinnon Ranch and a job he thrived in. Steve could outshoot anyone on the ranch with his quick draw that he practiced for days on end. He was one of the best riders, and wasn't afraid to tackle the hardest tasks, and the deadly Wyoming winters.

But did all that qualify him to take on the solution to Doctor McKinnon's contract problem? To Rebekah, Steve looked overly confident right now, pushing a little too hard to fit in his role as head wrangler.

Rebekah said nothing as Doctor McKinnon finished his own assessment, then reached out to shake Steve's hand.

"I'm counting on you, Steve. Get me twenty broke horses to drive in three weeks' time and there will be a nice bonus for all of you when you get back."

Steve grinned, his old self returning as he shook Doctor

McKinnon's hand like he was pumping a well. "You bet, Doc. That is, we'll get it done."

Doctor McKinnon pried his hand loose from Steve's, and shook it to get the blood flowing again. Rebekah chuckled and glanced toward the corral, wanting to offer Jimmy congratulations, but he was headed into the barn, rolling up the broken reins.

Laramie stood there, stroking the neck of the bay. His eyes met Rebekah's, but she didn't hold his gaze.

She quickly turned back to Steve and Doctor McKinnon.

"If you boys plan to break wild horses in the mountains, you're going to need a doctor to patch you up. I volunteer."

CHAPTER 4

There were mixed feelings in the bunkhouse that night. To Jimmy, it seemed there was a tug-of-war going on—half the men pulled one way, half the other.

On one side, men pulled for a change of scenery, a chance to leave the barnyard and riding fence in favor of freshness in the Medicine Bow Mountains. It was summer and the idea of mountain water and a cool breeze coming off the cliffs and pines sounded mighty good.

On the other side, some of the men didn't have a hankering to leave civilization for three weeks, not after they'd busted their backs busting and gentling so many horses. Mostly, they didn't want to miss their Saturday nights in town.

Jimmy wouldn't mind if they did. In fact, he was waiting for the right moment to ask some of the boys, especially Steve, if they'd like to read the Bible in the evenings with him. Not that Jimmy could read much yet, but he'd memorized one verse to get them started. Steve could read good, too, from what Jimmy heard.

As for the men splitting up for the trip, Jimmy knew he needed to stay close to the ranch house and Miss Rebekah. Who would look after her with Steve and many of the boys up in the mountains and Laramie taking the rest to Drybone?

But Jimmy didn't want to make his request public. The boys teased him about babysitting Miss Rebekah and how it was really her that babysat him.

It was a little of both. Jimmy and Doc Beck looked after each other and he didn't want that to ever change.

But it was Steve's decision and right then, Steve was in the middle of that virtual rope, holding up his hands and calling for everyone to quiet down and gather around the bunkhouse table.

Opposite the table was a row of bunk beds where the hands slept. Jimmy had a top cot at the very end where he sat, repairing the reins that broke on his fourth ride of the day. He was terribly sore, but didn't want the boys to hear him groaning under his breath whenever he moved.

When the boys didn't quiet down their good-natured arguments, Steve yanked off his hat and shook it at them. "Now listen up, all of you overpaid saddle tramps."

They finally quieted with a few chuckles. One of the men, tall and lanky Lucky Saunders, tossed back, "You still got a streak of greenhorn in you, Steve. Who died and made you boss?"

Steve pointed his hat at Saunders. "Doc McKinnon made me head wrangler, so you just quit flapping your jaws."

He tossed his hat, crown down, onto the table, then dug into his pocket and produced strips of paper. He tossed the strips in the hat.

"Now, everyone that draws a higher number than ten goes with me to the mountains. Under ten, Laramie takes with him or assigns them stay and keep the ranch running."

Lucky Saunders waved his hand like a schoolboy. Steve sighed, propping one foot on a chair. He rested his elbow on his knee, propping his chin on his fist.

"What is it, Saunders?"

"Suppose I draw the number ten?"

The other hands hooted with laughter. Jimmy smiled to himself as he used his pocket knife to carefully put a slit through the tough leather of the reins.

Steve slowly straightened, foot still propped on the chair. "Whoever draws ten gets to write, 'I ask dumb questions' one hundred times on the blackboard."

The boys howled with laughter. Lucky Saunders stuck his hands in his pockets with a playful scowl at Steve.

Jimmy finished the third slit in the reins. He twisted the leather into loops, then fed the other end of the reins into them and tightened it around the jingling bit.

"Hey Jimmy, you hoping to be a ten plus, or ten minus?"

Jimmy looked up, surprised one of boys addressed him as the drawing got underway.

He laid the reins on his bunk and slid off. There were whoops of delight as a few of them got the number they wanted, and groans when others didn't. The trading began, and the ranch hands converged on the hat like hungry dogs.

Jimmy had just reached the crowded table when the bunkhouse door swung open so hard it slammed into the wall.

He jumped out of the path of Stubby as the cook charged into the bunkhouse with a large pot held with wet mittens. The pot was boiling over, white foam spilling over the sides. Stubby marched to the table, pushing men aside with his elbows until he set the pot down with a plunk.

The men made a wide circle around him. Stubby narrowed his already squinty eyes as he swept his gaze around.

"All right, which one of you yahoos was messing around in my kitchen?"

Several looked at each other and at Steve, one of the chief jokesters on the ranch. Jimmy couldn't say that any of them looked guilty.

Stubby flung the soaked mitts on the table. He looked for all the world like a miniature grizzly bear with his short stature and his trail dusty hat, that he never took off except in church, covering his bristly brown and silver hair.

Stubby crossed his arms. "All right, you good for nothings, no one gets a bite of dinner until I find out who put soap in my pot of boiling eggs."

Steve jerked and then stilled, but not in time. Stubby planted his fists on his hips above his gun belt, something else he never took off except for church. He claimed it was to shoot any two-legged rattlesnakes that got too close to his cooking.

At the mention of boiling eggs, Jimmy frowned, but Stubby honed in on Steve. "I might've known it was you. You've caused me more trouble than any of these fellows combined. Well, you'll get your comeuppance when we get out in those mountains."

Jimmy stepped forward. It wasn't right for Steve to take the blame for something Jimmy had done.

"Mr. Stubby?" Jimmy's voice squeaked like a baby frog.

Stubby wheeled around, hands coming off his hips, one catching Jimmy in the gut.

"What!" Stubby shouted. Most everyone in the room took a step back.

Jimmy partly doubled over from his sore midsection and took a careful breath. "Mr. Stubby, I put a couple eggs in your pot after you told me you were short. That is, short on eggs."

A chuckle started around the room at the word *short*. Stubby drilled each man with his eyes, silencing them. But there was still a sense of restrained laughter. Stubby was a favorite to pull pranks on because it got him so worked up. Good for his heart, the boys said.

Jimmy figured that out in his first few days at the ranch. But he had learned long ago that it was never smart to rile the cook.

"But I don't know about soap in your pot, Mr. Stubby. Those eggs were pretty slick. Maybe they had cracks in them."

Jimmy didn't know what he said that was funny, but the room exploded with laughter.

Lucky Saunders doubled over, then rolled to the floor, kicking his stocking feet in the air and hooting. Others grabbed each other or the bunks for support as they laughed.

The only ones not laughing were Jimmy...and Stubby, who scowled.

Steve picked up his hat and placed it on his head, the leftover strips of paper fluttering to the floor. He pulled his hat down on his forehead, low over his eyes. He tilted his chin up, his hand partly covering his mouth, but it didn't hide his grin.

"You put those hatching eggs in Stubby's pot, did you, Jimmy?"

Stubby tossed his hands in the air, growling, "Oh, enough of you senseless, no good..." He grabbed the pot and marched out the door.

Jimmy shoved his hands in his pockets. "You said to check them eggs every day, Steve, and all but two of them had hatched. The hen quit sitting on them, and I figured it would be a shame to waste them." Where Jimmy came from, a body never wasted food.

The laughter died down as the boys watched Steve expectantly. Steve pushed his hat way up his forehead, allowing a puff of his fluffy hair to show.

"Well, Jimmy boy, I reckon eggs carved from bars of soap would have a mite of trouble with hatching."

The room erupted again, twice as loud as before. Lucky Saunders grabbed Jimmy's shoulders from behind, shaking him with laughter. Jimmy grinned tentatively, not sure whether to join in the laughter or cry from the jolting of his sore body and embarrassment.

But Steve hadn't meant any harm, and this sort of thing was expected in a bunkhouse.

One of the men held out his number. "Here you go, Jimmy. You've earned the number ten!"

The laughter started all over as Jimmy accepted the number.

He chuckled and shrugged. "I reckon now is as good a time as any to ask you boys if y'all want to join me reading the Bible tonight."

Boy, if Jimmy wanted to stop the laughing quick, he couldn't have picked a better thing to say.

Lucky Saunders gave him a final pat on the back and turned toward his bunk. The other fellows shuffled away, and started trading numbers again. Steve took off his hat and checked the lining as if to see if there were any numbers left.

Jimmy shuffled over to him, the table between them.

"How about you, Steve? You go to church regular. Don't hurt to read God's word all week long."

Steve ran his finger around the inside of his hat, staring at it. "Jimmy, you want all the boys to like you, don't you?"

He shrugged. It was Steve he really wanted to earn respect from. "I reckon."

Steve settled his hat on his head. "Then why don't you quit preaching at us all the time?"

Jimmy shifted his feet, searching his mind for something sensible to say. "I ain't no preacher—"

Steve interrupted, "You preach every day, always talking about church and the Bible. That's all well and good for Sundays, but we're men and we don't need that preached at us from one of our own."

"But Mr. Laramie is a real God-fearing man and he—"

"You leave the boss out of this!" Steve's shout got the attention of everyone in the bunkhouse. His face reddened and his eyes flashed.

Jimmy didn't know what to say, but turned out, he didn't need to do anything.

Through the open bunkhouse door strode Laramie Jones.

Suddenly, every ranch hand had something to occupy his hands—repairing gear or shuffling decks of cards—everyone except Jimmy and Steve, who stared at each other dumbly. After taking in the scene, Laramie slowly came over to them.

He ran a finger through the remnants of the soap suds then planted his palms on the table between Steve and Jimmy.

His gaze raised to Steve. "Want to tell me what all the ruckus is about on this fine evening?"

Steve stuck his tongue in his cheek, then smacked his lips. "No ruckus, Boss. Preacher Jimmy is just hard of hearing."

Jimmy gritted his teeth. "It's *just* Jimmy."

Laramie looked between the two, and Jimmy regretted his own fierceness. There were few men in the world he respected more than Laramie Jones. Steve did, too. Neither were acting like it now and that seemed plain silly.

Laramie straightened to his six-foot two height, the lantern over the table catching his full black hair with its dignified flecks of gray. He looked Steve square on.

"In all the fun you've been having this fine evening, did you pick out your wranglers yet?"

Lucky Saunders stepped forward to Steve's side with a light chuckle. "No need to worry, Boss, Steve got everything lined out. Don't you worry about a thing."

There was a murmur of agreement, but Laramie's gaze lingered on Steve. "You be sure Jimmy goes with you to break horses in the mountains."

Steve's head shot up. "He ought to stay here."

"We need our top wranglers up in those mountains, and that includes Jimmy."

Jimmy wasn't sure what he felt the most torn up about—going off and leaving Miss Rebekah, or the look of disgust Steve gave him.

✦

WITH THINGS quiet in the bunkhouse, Jimmy slipped out the door and headed for the foreman quarters. Lamplight through the window showed Laramie Jones sitting at his table. Jimmy softly tapped on the door.

"Come in."

Mr. Laramie sounded irritated. Jimmy hated to bother him, but he had a serious request to make. He went in, the cowhide rug muffling his hard boot heels. The stone fireplace was cold that summer evening, but could heat the whole cabin during the hard winters.

Laramie glanced up, then back at his papers. "What can I do for you, Jimmy?"

Jimmy stuffed his hands in his pockets. "Mr. Laramie, I know Steve needs good bronc busters up in the mountains, but I wanted to ask if I could stay here at the ranch."

Laramie looked up again, his gray eyes tinted with surprise. "I thought you liked working with the horses."

"Yes sir, I love those creatures. But it ain't that, it's more about where I need to be. That is, I don't want to leave Miss Rebekah here alone, what with you taking the main herd to Fort McKinney."

Laramie leaned back in his chair, tossing his pencil on the table. "I know what you mean, Jimmy."

Sadness settled over the face of this strong man, a man Jimmy figured could do just about anything and do it right.

Laramie shook his head and straightened. "We don't always get to pick and choose. We do what's right, what we have to do. For me, that's taking the herd to the fort, and for you it's going to the Medicine Bow Mountains. I'm counting on you, Just Jimmy."

He nodded. "I won't let you down, Mr. Laramie."

A smile cracked Laramie Jones' rugged features, chasing away the sadness. "As for Miss Rebekah, that's one reason I want you in the mountains, too. She's going along to doctor you boys if anyone gets hurt."

Jimmy felt his whole being explode with relief. "Miss

Rebekah's going? I'm sure glad to hear that. Miss Rebekah, she's like a sister to me."

"That so?"

Jimmy shrugged. "Well, one time I said she was like a ma, but she didn't take kindly to that."

Laramie chuckled. "I don't reckon she did."

Jimmy stared at the floor. "Sometimes trail dust is thicker than blood, ain't it, Mr. Laramie?"

There was silence and Jimmy lifted his eyes to see Laramie Jones staring at gold framed photographs on his mantel. Jimmy followed his gaze and saw a pretty picture of Miss Rebekah.

"It is, Jimmy. Sometimes it is."

CHAPTER 5

Each day over the past few weeks, the heat had increased. Rebekah wore a wide brimmed hat to protect herself from the sun as she rode with the McKinnon Ranch hands to the Medicine Bow Mountains.

She was riding her favorite McKinnon ranch horse in the midst of the best crew in the west, with dear Jimmy on his buckskin beside her and Steve on point, leading the caravan to the mountains. Stubby drove his chuckwagon in the rear.

In the pair ahead of Rebekah was Lucky Saunders. She caught his comment to the man riding next to him.

Lucky coughed. "A man would have to prime himself just to spit on day like this."

Jimmy cast a worried look her way and she smiled. She often, though lovingly, reprimanded Jimmy when he made innocent remarks about spitting and other terms not appropriate for parlor conversation.

Since the day she met Jimmy, she had seen in him a young man with so much potential. He needed someone to finish raising him and she had appointed herself the role. Now she wondered if God hadn't been working all along with the intention of saving Rebekah, not Jimmy.

But that posed a new problem. She couldn't imagine being able to pry Jimmy loose from her side, yet she knew the reservation was not a place he could belong. She needed to see Jimmy settled in his new home at McKinnon Ranch and ready to face life without her.

Tilting her head so the brim of her hat blocked the rising sun, Rebekah said, "It's all right, Jimmy. The boys aren't accustomed to having a lady around. But I'm sure you heard a lot of things at the ranches you've worked...like the Baxters. That wasn't the first ranch you worked at, was it?"

Jimmy shifted forward again, his worried expression changing from concern for her, to concern over the personal question. "No, ma'am. I worked a couple other outfits before that."

"You must have started very young since we just celebrated your sixteenth birthday."

Jimmy hesitated, then grinned. "That was awful good of you to let me pick a day to celebrate my birthday."

He paused, glancing at her from the corner of his eyes. "Was that foolish, ma'am? I mean, do men my age have birthday parties or is that just for kids?"

Rebekah held back another smile, reminding herself that Jimmy didn't see himself as a kid, hadn't for a long time. But he certainly earned his place in her eyes after risking his life more than once to save her.

"Not at all, Jimmy. Last winter, we threw Doctor McKinnon a birthday party. It was Christmastime, so we called it a Christmas party so he wouldn't fuss as much."

Jimmy's shoulders relaxed. "That sounds mighty fine. Wish I could've been there for it."

"Maybe you can help put another one together this year. I'm not certain I will still be here."

Jimmy twisted in the saddle toward her, eyes wide. He stuttered, "You...you ain't sick, are you, Miss Rebekah?"

Rebekah reached across the dusty distance between them and patted his shoulder. "No, Jimmy. But I might return to the Omaha Reservation soon to continue my work there."

Jimmy sighed, relieved. "I heard something about a senator of this new state helping you with something, but I didn't want to be nosy." He hesitated, then rushed through his next question. "All right if I ask what it was like growing up on an Indian reservation?"

Rebekah didn't answer right away, gazing off at the foothills and the Medicine Bow Mountains beyond them. This part of the country was laid out in a way that reminded her of the adjoining state of Nebraska that held her people within its boundaries.

How could she possibly describe the wealth of her childhood playground—herbs to pick, elders to learn from, the laughter of her family in their log cabin in what another faction of the Omaha called the 'village of the make-believe white men'?

In the 1840s, her father had adopted Chief Big Elk's philosophy that in order for their people to survive, they must advance by leaps and bounds, catching up with the European development of the times. It was why her father had pushed her so much to gain an education, to use her God-given intelligence for the good of their people.

Rebekah had never envisioned her life any other way than following his wisdom and serving her people with her life. Things hadn't quite turned out that way and it made the ache for her past, her people, and the near future burn bright hot in her heart.

"I hope I didn't ask something wrong, ma'am. I didn't mean no offense."

Jimmy's strained words brought Rebekah back to the present. She swallowed and said lightly, "You're too kind of a soul to ever offend anyone, Jimmy. You may speak something out of ignorance, but it's only hurtful when it's done intentionally."

She gathered her thoughts in one corner of her mind. "As to

your question, my home was like many others—our cabin had a large wood-burning fireplace where I learned to cook, there were meadows of wildflowers and rabbits to chase, and people who loved me."

Rebekah met Jimmy's caring eyes, showing he was open to learn. And maybe to share? She asked, "What about your home? What was it like?"

Jimmy's expression closed instantly. He faced forward again, his expression downcast for a heartbeat. Then he chuckled.

"Why, it was one adventure after another. I was once shipwrecked off the coast of Bermuda and spent my days on an island with a one-eyed pirate..."

Jimmy's voice faded, unable to spin a wild yarn like a dust devil. His shoulders slumped, hand dangling loose over the saddle horn. He rested his gloved hand on the horn, thumb rubbing the split reins.

"If it's all the same to you, Miss Rebekah, I'd rather not talk about it."

Rebekah nodded, though he wasn't looking at her. "Of course. But I want you to know, Jimmy, that you have a home at McKinnon Ranch. Whenever we part ways, you'll always be surrounded by family here."

Jimmy's head jerked up. "My home is wherever you are. I'll go with you to the reservation even."

The steepness of the trail increased. Steve urged his horse into a gallop to make the climb up the green hillside. The rest of the riders followed.

Rebekah decided not to pursue the conversation with Jimmy as she pushed her horse up to a gallop, feeling its powerful muscles carrying her up the hill.

For the moment, she avoided bruising Jimmy's heart by telling him there wouldn't be a place for him on the reservation. Besides, he belonged at the ranch. She needed to make him understand that. But it didn't need to happen in a day.

CHAPTER 6

It was freezing cold as Jimmy led his horse up a game trail out of Broke Leg Canyon. At least, it felt like winter compared to the ranch. It wasn't full daylight yet. A gray mist with tints of yellow touching it guided Jimmy up the path.

Yesterday, the crew arrived at an abandoned cabin near the canyon where they would corral and break horses. Jimmy had cleaned up the one bedroom in the cabin for Miss Rebekah, and the ranch hands set up canvas tents outside.

Jimmy had a lot of respect for all the boys, which made his assignment this morning as dreary as the gray mist.

While Stubby stirred up breakfast at the chuckwagon, Steve told Jimmy to grab a biscuit and scout the terrain to the west, looking for signs of the horse herd they were tracking. Jimmy didn't know why Steve sent him west. It was filled with cliff faces and old rock slides. Hardly a place a horse herd would meander about. They should search the valleys and river beds. But Jimmy didn't question Steve.

He had the chance to earn Steve's respect on this trip, and he started by showing Steve the respect he earned as head wrangler.

Maybe someday, Jimmy and Steve could have the kind of camaraderie that Steve and Laramie Jones shared.

Although if Jimmy was leaving for the Omaha Reservation with Miss Rebekah soon, did it matter?

That was getting into tall weeds of thinking for Jimmy. He put those aside in favor of concentrating on the loose rock footing of the trail shifting under his boots.

He'd known when they hit the trail that his horse wouldn't be able to navigate it safely with him on board, so he dismounted and started leading her up.

Him and this horse, they knew each other's ways and trusted one another. In the two years Jimmy had owned his buckskin Kate, after busting his tail to buy her, they were inseparable. Jimmy couldn't ask for a better partner.

It was a good thing he had her, because this trail was long and narrow. Too narrow for Jimmy to turn around and go back, so he kept fighting up the trail higher and higher, wondering what the drop on the other side was like.

But he didn't reach the top of the peak. The trail started downward and he kept following it, sure he was chasing Billy goats, not horses. He wondered again why Steve sent him that way. If they were on better terms, Jimmy would think Steve sent him on a wild goose chase as a way of teasing him. But Steve wasn't in a teasing mood.

Still, Jimmy was patient. He'd find a way to earn Steve's respect sooner or later. Just like this trail had to come to an end sooner or later.

It finally did.

The ground didn't level off all at once. Instead, boulders and broken trees littered the ground from an old rockslide. Patches of snow covered the rocks. The day was warming, and Jimmy touched the snow, marveling at the coldness while the sun warmed his cheek. He stuck his finger in, checking the depth.

Bent over like that, he felt something smack him on the back of the neck.

His gal Kate tossed her head and whinnied. Jimmy straightened as he rubbed the back of his neck. Then something struck him on the arm.

"Ouch!" Jimmy looked up the mountain in time to see a rock sailing for his head. He ducked and it clattered behind him. Another one flew at him.

"Hey there!" he shouted up the cliffside as he dodged the rock. "I'm friendly. Why don't you be?"

The flying rocks stopped. Jimmy cautiously raised up, scanning the cliffside with his eyes. There, among the rocks, a furry black and white muzzle poked out.

Well, that was a start. Jimmy clicked his tongue at the dog.

"There now, little fella, I don't mean you no harm."

A squeak sounded from the rocks. "That's not a fellow. That's a girl."

Jimmy rubbed the back of his neck where the rock hit. It still smarted. He answered, "Sounds like you are, too. My name's Jimmy. What's yours?"

A worn felt hat with a floppy brim poked out from the other side of the rock. The hat was settled on the head of a dirty faced little girl. Her stringy hair tumbled from beneath the hat. Her hair and face both needed a good washing.

Jimmy talked up to her over the distance of a dozen yards. "What's a little girl like you doing here in these mountains alone?"

Her eyes popped wide. "I'm not a little. I'm a medium. And I'm not alone, so you just stay right there, mister."

The collar on the man's jacket she wore moved. Someone behind the rock was tugging on her sleeve.

She hissed behind the rock, "He ain't hardly older than us."

Jimmy tied Kate to a broken branch. By the time he straightened again, the girl and the dog had multiplied by two.

A boy even littler than her had scooted out on his knees, arms wrapped around the black and white long-haired dog's neck. Another boy had climbed atop the rock and was squatted, a fist-sized rock in each hand, looking ready to throw them both at Jimmy.

Jimmy held his hands up. "Seeing as how you've got the drop on me, I reckon it's your move."

The boy scowled. "You could blast us all to kingdom come with that six-shooter. But I'd get one or two good throws at you, so you just stay put, mister, like my sister said."

He nodded at the girl who began slipping and sliding down the old rockslide. The little boy and dog followed and finally, the boy with the rocks made his way down, keeping a wary eye on Jimmy. When they reached the bottom, they stood a good twenty feet from Jimmy, posed to either fight or flee.

Jimmy used one of his raised hands to scratch the back of his head, pushing his hat up and forward to shade his eyes. "Well, if you're highwaymen, I got nothing worth stealing. Just a good horse that can show you how you're supposed to say, 'how do you do' to someone."

The boy on his knees with arms wrapped around the dog, lifted a little, curious.

Jimmy slowly lowered his hands and untied Kate. "Now watch close."

He got in position before Kate as she bobbed her head, showing off her black mane that fell over her buckskin neck. He offered one hand, low.

"Shake."

Kate lifted her hoof and placed it in Jimmy's palm. He said over his shoulder, "Now that's how you're supposed to greet a stranger, like you want them to be your friend."

Jimmy shook Kate's hoof up and down then lowered it to the ground.

He turned back to the three kids. "See? That's not so bad, is it?" He stuck out his hand across the distance, giving them a chance to close it.

The girl moved first, shuffling forward. She gripped Jimmy's hand with hers that felt like it got plenty of exercise from milking. She squeezed hard and he winced, going down on one knee so that he was eye-level with her short height from his overgrown tallness.

"I didn't get your name, sweetheart?"

The girl gave his hand a downward sling away from her. "My name is Wayne-Willie, and don't call me sweetheart."

Jimmy massaged his hand. "Sorry about that, ma'am. Where I come from, down Texas way, that's just how we talk."

She narrowed her eyes suspiciously at him, but the littlest boy was edging forward on his knees, using the dog, a collie, as a crutch.

He reached up and Jimmy took his tiny hand and shook it gently. "What's your name?"

The boy with the rocks in his fists answered, "He's Willie-Roy, and he don't talk. We were all born at the same time, and I reckon God made him that way so people could tell us apart."

The boy finally dropped his rocks and strode forward, wiping his hands on his trousers that boasted a hole in each knee. He stuck his hand out and shook Jimmy's stoutly. "I'm Willie-Wayne Palmer."

Jimmy looked between the three kids—triplets—thoroughly confused. "I thought Willie was her name?" He nodded to the girl.

The boy shrugged. "That's how our uncle calls us, when he's sober, least ways. When he ain't, he calls us different things all together."

Jimmy pushed his hat back, scratching his forehead. The girl spoke up.

"Whatever you hear our second name is, that's our real name, most of the time."

Jimmy pointed at each one in turn. "So, you're Willie, you're Wayne, and this here is Roy."

Jimmy scratched the dog behind the ears as Roy clung to her. Willie, the girl, said, "That there is Valor, on account of she's so brave and teaches us how to be brave, too. She takes care of our sheep."

Wayne grabbed Willie by her coat shoulder. "You ain't supposed to tell no one about the sheep!"

As if on cue, a loud *baa* sounded from around the corner of the cliff. Valor barked and darted away from Roy, running in the direction of the bleating. Roy scrambled up and followed, along with Willie and Wayne.

Jimmy gathered Kate's reins and followed the three and their guard dog through the debris to where the country opened up into a grassy meadow. There was no sign of any horses, but a sheep herd spread out in the meadow, grazing contently.

The collie trotted among them as though taking inventory. She circled at the end of the herd and came to a stop, putting her nose in the wind and taking several sniffs.

The triplets came to a tumbling halt at the edge of the herd. Willie glanced back as Jimmy caught up.

"See, mister?" she said. "These are our sheep, only Uncle Rufus says they're his now that we belong to him. But someone's been stealing them and so we ain't supposed to tell strangers where they are. You ain't planning on stealing our sheep, are you, mister?"

Jimmy ran the reins through his gloved hands, trying to take in everything the girl rattled off. Where was this Uncle Rufus?

"No, Willie, I ain't gonna steal your sheep," he said. "I'm here looking for horses. Oh. And it's just Jimmy."

CHAPTER 7

It was no small trick getting back to the McKinnon camp. Jimmy felt like a circus act as he balanced little Roy on his horse's neck in front of the saddle horn while Wayne held onto Jimmy's waist from behind. Willie hugged her brother from behind the saddle where she rode on the horse's rump.

Kate had never carried four astride, but with how light the triplets were, she had no trouble packing them through the mountain. The terrain was a lot easier than the way Jimmy came, following a wide-open path the kids told him about. They needed an easy trail for the rest of the circus caravan that Jimmy couldn't be prouder of.

After their initial standoffishness, the kids warmed up to him, even Wayne, who declared himself the oldest of the triplets. He told Jimmy there were a pack of men stealing their sheep to eat. When Wayne was convinced Jimmy wasn't one of them, he took Jimmy to a small canyon, like a natural corral, where a half dozen horses grazed.

Jimmy was as happy as a hog in a mud wallow, especially when he saw the collie had no trouble nosing the horses out and driving them, same as she was doing through the woods and toward the

McKinnon camp. They were also driving the sheep because the kids couldn't leave them unprotected, or their uncle would tear into them again.

Between Kate and the dog, it was slow going but not too difficult to keep the caravan together all the way to the camp.

The McKinnon crew had been busy that day, too. They erected three temporary corrals—one for the remuda, one for cornering the new horses, and one for breaking them.

Jimmy couldn't help sitting up real straight as his circus paraded through the camp. The men chuckled and made an alleyway for them. Miss Rebekah came out of the cabin and outright laughed at the sight of Jimmy with three kids hanging on to Kate and the dog nosing the sheep and horses into the empty corral.

Careful not to dislodge Roy, Jimmy leaned down to grab the end of the temporary gate and lifted it. He maneuvered Kate to sidestep as they swung the gate closed. Jimmy looped the leather latch over the post to secure the new livestock inside the corral.

Applause and whistles sounded behind Jimmy as he turned Kate around, grinning. Even Stubby, next to his chuckwagon, stopped stirring the contents in the pot over his open fire. He put his hands backwards on his hips, spoon dripping behind him.

Rebekah came to Jimmy's horse and held her hands up to little Roy, offering to help him down. The boy hesitated, but when Jimmy lifted him from behind, he was as limp as a wet dishrag. Roy let himself be handed down to the strange woman.

Rebekah lowered him to stand beside her. "Well, Just Jimmy, it seems you've rounded up quite a bit for a day's work."

Jimmy's grin faded when he noticed Steve standing at the corner of the porch, leaned against one of the posts, arms crossed. The boss man was frowning.

Jimmy offered his arm to Wayne, who grabbed it and slid down the side of Jimmy's leg to the ground. "These young'uns showed me where to find the horses and helped herd them back. I asked them where their home was, and they said they didn't have one of those."

Willie used his arm to climb down like her brother, landing with a thump in the dusty yard as Miss Rebekah kept her arm around Roy's shoulder. The boy had wrapped his arms around her waist and didn't look like he planned on letting go anytime soon.

While the ranch hands went to the corral to admire the first six horses they had to break, Jimmy swung down from the saddle.

"Miss Rebekah, this here is Wayne, Willie, and Roy. Roy, he don't talk and I was hoping maybe you could figure out why."

To the kids, he said, "This is Miss Rebekah LaRoche. Lots of folks call her Doc Beck, on account of she's a doctor."

Willie stared up at the woman with gaped-mouth admiration, Wayne with hesitant trust. Roy buried his grimy face in her clean shirtwaist.

Rebekah stroked his oily hair, fingering the loose strands. "It's lovely to meet all of you. Are you hungry? Stubby has some corn-bread inside on the table."

The sunken faces of the kids lit up, even little Roy who looked like he might be willing to release Rebekah for food.

Jimmy's stomach growled, causing Miss Rebekah to laugh again.

"You, too, Jimmy."

But before they could move, a roar sounded from just beyond the bounds of the camp. A couple of the men went for their rifles, prepared for a bear or a mountain lion attack.

That wasn't what they got, but Jimmy had a feeling they might have liked that better.

A grizzly man charged into the camp, his hair so greasy it slicked back like it was glued. He stumbled in his mismatched boots, his trousers held up by suspenders pulled over his undershirt.

The man pointed a finger at Jimmy. "You sheep thief! I'll kill you with my bare hands."

As he stumbled forward, Lucky Saunders and two of the other hands stepped up, barring him from Jimmy with rifles across his chest.

Lucky clicked his tongue. "Whoa there, mister. I reckon you've got the wrong camp. We're just here rounding up a few horses and your sheep got caught up with them. Little Bo Peep here will see that they get back to your place, wagging their tales behind them."

The man shoved against the rifles blocking him, but to no avail. He stretched his arm between the men, pointing at the kids who shrank back against Rebekah and Jimmy.

"You three!" he thundered. "Get them sheep and my dog back to the meadow before I take a strap to all of you."

The kids jumped into action before Jimmy could move. They ran for the corral and threw the gate open, Wayne shouting at the dog to round up the sheep. Valor sprang forward, going after the whole herd, horses and all.

The horses panicked at the sudden movements and pushed against one another. They finally shot through the open gate and galloped away despite the wranglers who waved their arms in front of them, trying to direct them back to the corral.

It was no use. The horses scattered and ran for the woods, disappearing.

Meanwhile, Valor had the sheep collected and was nosing them across the yard as if they were the only creatures on the planet. They were oblivious to the tense standoff between Jimmy, Lucky Saunders, and what must be the kids' uncle Rufus Palmer.

From across the sheep herd where he was by the porch, Steve shouted, "Saunders, take the boys and get those horses back here!"

Lucky Saunders gave Rufus a warning look before pushing off him with his rifle and headed for the remuda, the other men following.

Jimmy braced, nothing between him and the enraged uncle.

But Rufus struck him as a man who was all hat and no cattle. He looked lost now. The sheep had already passed through the yard, the dog and the kids chasing after them into the woods.

Rufus swung his arms wide to indicate the whole camp. "I don't know who you people are, but stay away from me and mine. I catch you near my sheep again, I'll shoot you right between the eyes."

He took a stumbling step back, then staggered out of the camp, following the trail in a zigzag pattern until he finally disappeared from sight.

Jimmy blew out a big breath. "What we gonna do, Miss Rebekah? Those kids need help."

Miss Rebekah opened her mouth to reply, but it was Steve whose words came out next. He strode over to them.

"Just what did you think you were doing, Jimmy? Bringing that man's sheep here, making it look like we're rustlers."

Jimmy started to respond but Steve snapped, "You want to do your best for Doc McKinnon, don't you?"

Jimmy nodded.

"Then you do your best to stay out of the way, will ya?"

Steve pushed past Jimmy and headed for the saddle horses to join in the hunt for the escapees.

Jimmy stood, feeling like a herd of longhorns just stampeded over him.

CHAPTER 8

Things settled down by evening. Lucky Saunders and the other hands caught the runaway horses and secured them in the temporary corral. Steve announced half the men would start breaking them in the morning while the other half went to round up more.

He didn't say whether Jimmy would be in the breaking group or the rounding up group, and Jimmy didn't ask. He just wanted to eat his dinner in peace as the crew sat around the campfire near the chuckwagon where Stubby dished out bowls of beef stew and honey-sweetened cornbread.

One thing about Stubby—he was cantankerous, but kept them stuffed to the gills, always saying how they wouldn't get a lick of work done if it wasn't for him.

Jimmy settled on a dead log apart by himself, even away from Miss Rebekah who stood by the chuckwagon, using the tailgate as a table. Steve was the only one missing from camp, messing around in the cabin, likely doing boss man things.

To Jimmy's dismay, Lucky nodded his direction. "I hear tell, Jimmy, that you're thinking of trying out for that Donavan Brothers Circus that's coming to town."

Jimmy winced, not in the mood for teasing, especially in front of Miss Rebekah. But he did pull a dumb act with those horse, sheep, and kids. No wonder Steve got mad.

As he scooped up a bowl for the last man, Stubby piped up, "Y'all leave the boy alone. He done more work than all of you put together. Besides, he's got *two* tickets to the circus, and he just might treat one of you."

Lucky jabbed the man next to him with his elbow. "If Jimmy takes anyone to the circus, it better be that sassy Daphne Peele. She sure was giving him the eye back at the ranch."

Jimmy jumped to his feet, cornbread tumbling off his knee, and nearly dumped his bowl of stew. "She weren't either!"

Lucky waved his hand in the air, dismissing Jimmy's objection. "Don't you worry, Preacher Jimmy. It's not the girl you got to watch out for. It's her pa. He starts looking sideways at you, the time has come that you have to get married...or buried."

The boys around the campfire hooted and another chimed in, "I hear it's best for a preacher to get married before he takes on his own church."

Jimmy slowly settled on the log again, picking up his cornbread. He blew off the bits of dried leaves that stuck to the buttered crumbs.

He mumbled, "It's *just* Jimmy."

Miss Rebekah picked up her bowl and swept through the men around the campfire. They scooted one side or the other allowing her room, eyes downcast as she drilled them with her no-nonsense look. Someone mentioned about getting up a game of cards and was quickly shushed.

She made her way over and settled on the log next to Jimmy, her bowl between them.

"How are you feeling, Jimmy?" she asked quietly.

He rolled his head from one side to the other, stretching out soreness that he didn't figure would ever go away. "I'm not bad for how many horses I broke this week, I reckon."

Her voice went lower. "I asked, how are you feeling?"

Jimmy sighed, using one hand to crumble his cornbread in his stew. "I'm worried about them kids, is all."

"Are you sure?"

"I ain't been too sure of anything in this life, Miss Rebekah, except that the Good Lord is always looking out for me." He dropped his gaze. "I reckon that's why the boys call me Preacher Jimmy."

Rebekah patted his arm. "That's not a bad nickname to have."

Jimmy didn't much want to talk about it anymore, so he asked, "Miss Rebekah, how much did those circus tickets cost?"

She huffed, but her overly prim look told Jimmy she was teasing. "You should never ask what a birthday present cost, young man."

He drew his spoon through his stew, letting the cornbread soak in the juice. "The reason I'm asking is, I'd like to save up enough to buy them three kids a ticket. Bet they've never been to anything like that in their lives."

Rebekah sighed, and Jimmy felt some of his hope seep out.

"Jimmy, we will do what we can to help those children, but I wouldn't get your heart set on things like taking them to the circus."

Jimmy bit his lower lip. "Just thought it would be nice for them to go."

He'd never been to anything like that in his life.

CHAPTER 9

The trail felt even colder this morning than yesterday. At least, it seemed that way to Jimmy. Maybe it had less to do with the stout wind blowing in the day, and more to do with Steve's stinging words earlier.

Instead of breaking the new horses or going out with the other men to round up more, Steve told Jimmy to get lost in the mountains. Said he didn't want him around the horses or the camp or the chickens, if they had any. They didn't need any soap soup—and Steve wasn't smiling when he said it.

There weren't any horses on this side of the mountain. Jimmy knew that from his excursion with the triplets. The six they showed him in the canyon had been separated from the main herd and there were no more to be found in their neck of the woods.

Be that as it may, as Miss Rebekah often said, there *was* something he needed to find, and Jimmy planned to find it.

He guided his horse down the trail cut by sheep and the kids the day before, and pulled Kate up short when the mess of prints split. Paw prints and several sets of boots went one direction, and the shuffling of one set of boots went another.

Rufus.

Jimmy turned his horse to follow the single set.

It wasn't long and the trail broke open. A rundown cabin came into view. Jimmy halted Kate beside the sagging porch where two stumps served as steps. He didn't need those as he dismounted straight onto the porch, and went to the open doorway.

He peered inside and immediately spotted Rufus, slumped in a chair, his back to Jimmy. Tin cup in hand, a whiskey bottle sat close to Rufus' other hand that rested limp on the table.

Though Jimmy's lanky frame blocked a chunk of the morning sun, there was still plenty to shed light on the shoddy inside. He didn't even see a place for the kids to sleep aside from a cot that was covered over with dirty shirts and a crushed felt hat.

He felt like taking that hat and pulling it down over Rufus' ears before throwing the man headfirst in the mountain snow.

Jimmy clomped into the cabin and came around the table to stand in front of Rufus Palmer. The man finally realized the close threat, and flung his arm back, sending his tin cup sailing into the wall. Whiskey splattered.

Rufus stared at Jimmy with glassy eyes, looking like he thought he was going to die that moment. If Jimmy was a different man, he would say this no-good deserved it.

He crossed his arms, planting his feet apart as he glared at Rufus.

"What kind of man are you? Sitting around here like a drunk fool, making them little kids do your work. You're a good for nothing tramp that don't deserve a family."

The words boiled up from deep inside Jimmy, and he couldn't say where they came from. But, if he were honest with himself, he knew exactly where they came from.

He sucked in a big breath, ready to light into Rufus like a blue streak of greased lightning.

But his spirit wouldn't let him.

Jimmy let the big breath out and took another one before

saying, "But the fact is, you do got a family and it's your God-given responsibility to look out for them. A real family...that's as rare as double yoked eggs."

Rufus blinked several times. Then he planted his fists on the table and pushed himself up, arms shaking. But that didn't take away from the powerful anger in his eyes.

"You've got mighty big ideas for such a small head."

In a flash, Jimmy envisioned his head between the man's bear paws, crunching him like an empty pecan shell. And Jimmy had put himself in a position where the man was between him and the door.

Jimmy might have bought more than he could pay for this time.

He gulped and stuttered, "Well, I—I just came to tell you to treat them kids right."

Rufus' muscles bunched right before he launched across the table at Jimmy. Jimmy jumped back as Rufus flipped the table, sending the whiskey bottle to the floor.

Rufus cussed and, while he was bent on saving the liquid from spilling out, Jimmy leapt the overturned table and dashed through the door. He bolted onto Kate's back, his head barely clearing the porch roof.

Landing hard in the saddle, he wheeled Kate away, taking off at a gallop. They didn't slow until they were a half a mile from the cabin. He pulled Kate to walk then a stop, looking around.

Jimmy wasn't entirely sure where he was. But that didn't really matter. Steve wanted him to get lost for the day and that was just what Jimmy had done.

He walked Kate in a slow circle, cooling her from the run while he took in the landmarks. He spotted a trail leading to a higher point. Maybe he could get a good look around and see a path back to the McKinnon camp.

Jimmy nudged his horse, but she could only make it halfway up the trail. He dismounted and tied the reins to a limb before climbing the rest of the way on foot, the rocks rolling beneath his cowboy boots. They weren't the best footwear for climbing a mountain. Moccasins would be better suited, ones he imagined Miss Rebekah wore back on the Omaha Indian Reservation. Maybe he could get a pair himself if he moved there with her.

After slipping and sliding, he finally made it to a ledge where there was a bowl-like pocket. It was the kind one could curl up in and be completely cut off from the world and its troubles. An escape from the tough parts of life.

That was a good feeling, but Jimmy knew it wasn't for him. God meant for him to be out in the world, telling others about the Lord Jesus. But that was awful hard with people like Uncle Rufus, and even the ranch hands.

Jimmy crawled up one of the rocks forward of the bowl and took a peek over top.

Joy exploded in his heart at the green vista out there saying a great big, wide *howdy* to him. He could see clean for miles, the blend of cottonwoods and lodgepole pines, a river farther in the distance cutting through the valley.

Jimmy rested his chin on his crossed hands as he drank in the view. So untouched by human hands.

But something coming out of the woods below proved him wrong.

CHAPTER 10

The racket of the bronc riders kept Rebekah company in the cabin where she worked on a sewing project. She wasn't a talented seamstress, but she didn't want to spend three weeks just waiting for someone to get hurt and need her.

Besides, she had wanted to stitch the shirt for a while. It was made with dark red trade cloth, similar to one she had made for her father many years ago. He was buried in it.

Rebekah didn't have anyone to gift this shirt to yet, she only liked to have items on hand to gift, hopefully when she returned to the reservation. She was following the pattern and size as the one for her father.

Maybe she did know who she was stitching for.

There was one man she could give it to on the reservation. Her heart ached to see him, one of her few blood relations.

But at the moment the shirt was merely a distraction, as she observed Steve, who she could see through the open door. He sat on the steps of the cabin porch, a worried look on his face as he rolled his hat in his hands, elbows resting on his knees. He stared at the corrals.

She'd overheard Steve's conversation earlier with one of the hands who rode up from McKinnon Ranch with bad news: ten horses another rancher promised Dr. McKinnon were unsuitable and wouldn't be added to the herd. That left them ten horses shorter on the contract. Dr. McKinnon sent word, requesting Steve get an extra ten.

The message didn't need to include the embarrassment Doctor McKinnon would suffer if he didn't fulfill the contract, despite the challenges outside his control.

It was intense pressure on the new head wrangler. After giving him time to soak in the news, Rebekah set aside the half-finished shirt and moved into the freshness of the mountains, breathing deep of the invigorating air. She settled on the porch step beside Steve and waited for him to speak first.

Steve swallowed, his Adam's apple bobbing. "I don't think I can do it, Miss Becka. I think I'm going to fail everyone and everything."

The typically confident, jovial Steve rarely let anyone see this part of him. She doubted anyone had since she first met him in Denver.

She folded her hands together, glancing at the corral where three of the hands struggled to get a saddle on a bronc. From what she'd observed, they weren't making good progress with breaking the wilder horses. She turned back to the young man, one of those "strays" she'd brought to the McKinnon Ranch.

"Steve, do you remember when those cowboys were making you dance on the depot platform when you first arrived in the west?"

Steve grimaced, still turning his hat round and round. "Could never forget it, ma'am. If you hadn't took me in, I wouldn't be where I am, or even who I am."

"Then will you listen close to what I tell you now?"

His eyes darkened. "If it's about that boy..."

Rebekah cocked her head, not interrupting. Steve fell silent, his hands stilling on his hat.

She went on. "It does pertain to Jimmy, but it's really about you. I know Laramie Jones is giving Jimmy special attention. The reason is the same as we did with you, Steve. You were such a greenhorn. Jimmy has had more experience in the west, but he's still a boy, and Laramie is helping him transition into manhood. Jimmy looks up to you, and I would take it very kindly if you helped, too. Won't you give him a chance?"

When Steve didn't answer, didn't flinch, she sighed. "At the very least, he's one of the best riders you have, and if you don't want to let everyone down, I suggest you start using him."

Steve began spinning his hat again. "Like you said, he's just a boy. If he got hurt, I'd be responsible, and I don't reckon you or Laramie would take kindly to that."

Rebekah plucked Steve's hat from his hand and used it to point at him. "That's a poor excuse, and you know it. Now, will you please at least *try* to be friendly to Jimmy?"

Steve opened his mouth to respond, but a shout interrupted them. They both stood, and Rebekah groaned inwardly to see the triplets' uncle, Rufus Palmer, barreling into the camp again. He looked twice as mad as before, if that were possible.

Steve's hand dropped to the six-gun on his hip, unhooking the leather hammer loop. But Rufus wasn't armed and didn't look too dangerous. Steve settled down and propped his hand over the pistol.

Rufus shouted again, his slurred words indiscernible as he came straight for Steve.

Steve called out, "Something we can do for you, sir?"

Rufus halted and slung his hat to the ground, taking a staggering sidestep. "You've been stealing my sheep again! I just come from my herd and I'm missing five."

Steve set his jaw. "You better watch shooting your mouth off, mister. None of us been stealing anything from you."

Rufus swung around in a circle, nearly losing his balance. "Where's that kid that took off with my property yesterday? Seems he likes to wander on his own a lot."

Rebekah took a step forward, her agitation flaring into defense. "Jimmy would no more steal your sheep than I would. Perhaps they wandered off; I understand you don't spend much time with them."

Rufus shook a finger at her, spittle spraying from his mouth. "You mind your own knittin', lady."

To Steve, he said, "I catch any of your boys near my sheep or my dog, I'll blast you all, and don't think I won't."

Rufus stomped away, barely able to keep his wobbly legs under him.

Rebekah didn't doubt he would fire at whatever came near his cabin. She just hoped he didn't hit anything with those poor children around.

The triplets were a project she could take on during her time in the mountains, but she needed to ask Jimmy more about his original encounter and where the children lived.

She only hoped he didn't set his heart on rounding them up as strays as she often did. He was still somewhat of a stray himself.

CHAPTER 11

Through the twilight hours, Jimmy tossed and turned in the canvas tent he shared with two other ranch hands. He couldn't stop thinking about those kids sleeping in the cold mountains, and their sorry uncle. But mostly, he couldn't get the sight of men making a fireless camp out of his mind. They'd been too far away for Jimmy to see their faces, but he could tell they weren't hunters. They weren't prospectors. They weren't horse wranglers.

They were up to no good.

Jimmy thought of what Miss Rebekah told him when he found his way back to the ranch camp. Rufus accused Jimmy of stealing sheep again.

Whether or not those men were the sheep rustlers Jimmy didn't know, but he planned to keep an eye out for them the next day. What would he be doing anyway?

Steve didn't tell Jimmy. The boys had caught the main herd of horses and had them in the temporary corral. Jimmy could hear those horses now, restlessly exploring their confinement. Jimmy had spent most of the evening sitting on the top rail of the corral, observing their wildness and royal beauty.

Boy, he wanted to gentle them! But so far, Steve hadn't said anything about Jimmy being one of the bronc busters. That was something else wearing on his mind and keeping him awake.

There was no sense in laying there, listening to the other men snore to beat the band.

Jimmy crawled out the tent with his boots in one hand, coat draped over his arm, and closed the flap behind him to block out the glare of the full moon. Nothing riled a working man quite like getting his sleep disrupted when he had another hard day ahead.

Jimmy pulled on his boots then headed for the corrals as he pulled his suspenders over his long johns and slipped his coat on. He went to the remuda first.

They'd normally be standing in the back corner, sleeping contently. But tonight, several paced the corral, ears flicking back-and-forth and eyes on their neighbors, the wilder herd that was kicking up dust as they trotted around and around, occasionally stopping to sniff a corner post, the scent of man permeating the air.

Kate meandered over to the fence and Jimmy gave her nostrils a rub with his knuckles. "Can't sleep either, huh, girl? Something's afoot tonight. I can feel it, too."

He stayed with his horse, drawing comfort in her soft breathing as she laid her head over his shoulder and he wrapped his arms around her neck.

They stayed that way a while until Kate pulled her head back, nose in the air. She looked up the cliff that served as two sides of the corral. She pawed the ground and tossed her head. The other saddle horses frisked up.

The stallion of the wild herd reared and struck the air with his hoofs, his majestic silhouette caught by the moon.

Jimmy froze at the sight and the rumbling beneath his feet. But this wasn't the erratic rumble of horses dancing. This was a steady, rising shake.

The stallion reared again and beyond his silhouette, Jimmy

could see dark forms bouncing down the cliff. He gaped, trying to find his tongue.

He finally did and shouted, "Rockslide!"

The shout caught the attention of the night guards, who dashed through the camp, echoing it again and again.

"Rockslide! Rockslide!"

Jimmy couldn't move, but he had to. The rushing rock river was coming straight down to the corrals.

He ran to the remuda's gate and fumbled with the leather latch. He got it off and pulled the gate free, then gave it a mighty shove away from him to open it wide while he turned and ran for the other gate.

But the herd was already pressing against the flimsy gate. They would crush Jimmy if he didn't get out of the way in time. There wasn't much time for that.

Jimmy undid the latch and ran as fast as his long legs would carry him. The crash of the first rocks striking the corral and horseflesh raised the hair on the back of his neck. He glanced over his shoulder to see the herd jostling through the gate, taking down the post on each side as they ran for freedom. The saddle horses were still dashing out as the rock river engulfed the corrals.

The whole camp was in an uproar. Some of the men ran toward the horses, trying to stop them, not realizing what was going on. Others ran for the woods as boulders ricocheted off one another, pieces splintering and striking the canvas tents nearest the corrals.

Jimmy stumbled onto the porch of the cabin, heaving in great gulps of air.

Miss Rebekah was on the porch, robe wrapped around her nightgown. She grabbed him by the arm and pulled him to the wall of the cabin as she watched the rockslide. She spoke above the panic, "It's all right, Jimmy, you're in the clear."

Jimmy leaned against the wall, eyes closed like he was on a bucking bronc. "The other fellows, everyone all right?"

When Rebekah didn't answer, Jimmy opened his eyes to see she had disappeared. She reemerged from the cabin and, medical bag in hand and robe lifted high enough to reveal her bare feet, she ran across the yard. Jimmy took in the sight before him in the moon-splashed camp.

Debris filled both corrals and boulders had knocked down a canvas tent. It seemed impossible that the stable-looking mountainside had come toppling down...without some kind of help.

Lucky Saunders and other men with lanterns were checking the debris where one man sat, head cradled in his hands. Lucky gave a shout and the other men came running. They began digging in the rocks.

Steve hollered for a headcount and Jimmy pushed away from the wall. Once his feet got moving, he was running to the gathering men.

By the time he arrived, Lucky and the others had pulled one of the wranglers out and onto his feet. He cradled a bloody arm but at least he was alive.

Steve bounced from man to man, counting by the light of his lantern. He halted when he saw Jimmy and closed his eyes briefly.

"Didn't see you in the first count. Thought you were buried."

"I'm all right, Steve."

Lucky Saunders dusted off the man they pulled from the rocks while Miss Rebekah examined his bloody arm.

Lucky piped up, "Jimmy's more than all right, Steve. He's the one that sounded the alarm. If it hadn't been for him, all the boys in those tents would be buried under the rocks."

Steve turned to Jimmy, meeting his eyes with a look of respect. He nodded acknowledgment, and Jimmy received it with a shrug. Then Steve swung his lantern around at the other boys and started giving orders.

He designated men for cleanup, resetting the corrals, helping Stubby stir up biscuits and coffee for the late-night work, and assisting the injured inside the cabin where Rebekah could treat them.

From what Jimmy could see, there were two men who would be out of commission for the rest of the trip.

After everyone started their assigned duties, Jimmy stepped up to Steve.

"Want me to track the horses? There's a good chance our remuda and the wild herd are running together. But if I know my girl, she'll break away and come back to me soon."

Steve rubbed his jaw, two days of growth on his normally smooth face. He looked like he'd aged a few years in his short time as boss.

"Get some rest, Jimmy. Looks like you're going to be busting broncs double-time from here on out."

CHAPTER 12

Never in all his born days had Jimmy been so plain tuckered out. He'd gone from the bottom of Steve's wrangler list straight to the top.

With two of the hands down with injuries and others hunting an extra ten horses they needed for the contract, Jimmy found himself working with the horses constantly.

They didn't even take a rest on Sundays, though Jimmy didn't want to work on the Sabbath. Steve justified it with a scripture about the Lord saying when the ox was in the ditch, the owner had to work to get it out, even on the Sabbath. Miss Rebekah confirmed that, though she didn't look too happy.

Jimmy did reckon the McKinnon ranch hands' ox was in the ditch. They were running out of time to get the horses gentled and herded off the mountain.

Still, even all the work hardly took Jimmy's mind off those kids. The first week in the mountains, Jimmy and Miss Rebekah tried to find the kids in the late evenings to take them food, but they never saw hide nor hair of the triplets, even in their meadow. After that, Jimmy just didn't have time to go hunting for them and keep up with his job.

But no matter how hard everyone worked, they were still behind. Jimmy wasn't highly educated, but he could do math good and that told him the number of days left and the number of unbroken horses didn't add up to good news.

Steve knew it, too, and wore a constant frown as the days ticked away.

Each of those days, Jimmy was up before daylight, gentling horses, training to saddles and bridles, and grooming the burrs out of their tails.

Their independent streak gave them extra strength. Jimmy didn't want to damage that spirit or get his back broken, so he spent as much time as he could with the horses, letting them get used to him before throwing a saddle on them. Not all the hands agreed with his method, said it was too slow.

He shouldn't have been surprised when, three days before their scheduled pull-out time, Steve announced they'd leave the next morning and finish breaking the rest of the horses on the trail.

It sounded like a bad idea, but Jimmy didn't have an alternative one. He did his best with the other wranglers to get the horses ready for the move.

The morning they were to pull out, everyone had breakfast before dawn. Miss Rebekah got her patients ready to ride, though she told Steve they would need to take it slow.

Jimmy didn't see a problem with that. Leading a herd of semi-broke horses out of the Medicine Bow Mountains was going to be tricky and costly, time-wise.

Stubby complained about no one helping him pack his chuckwagon as the men dumped canvas tents beside it for loading. Jimmy couldn't break away from the corral, where he was saddling horses in the remuda. He was close enough to hear Stubby grumble and curse as he crammed tents in the wagon.

As the first streaks of dawn cast a pale light over the camp,

Steve mounted and circled his hand above his head. "Let's roll 'em out!"

Jimmy swung aboard Kate, holding in a groan at the pain in his body. But the sound of a shotgun ripping through the trees caused him to freeze. The semi-broke horses still in the corral panicked and reared.

Another shot sounded. Pine needles and pebbles rained down on Jimmy.

Buckshot.

He yanked his rifle from the scabbard along with several of the other men, and he looked to see where Miss Rebekah was. He would never let anything happen to her unless he was dead.

Stubby yanked his shotgun from the back of his chuckwagon while nudging Miss Rebekah to the safety of the other side of the wagon. Jimmy saw she had her medical bag. She was armed and out of the line of fire.

Steve drew his six-gun and wheeled his horse around to view the clearing behind the camp.

Rufus Palmer stood there, looking decently sober. He held a double-barreled shotgun, and was jamming two more shells in. He snapped it closed as Steve, six-gun aimed up, hollered, "What do you think you're doing, mister?"

Rufus barked, "I come to stop some no-good rustlers."

Jimmy stayed back in the pines, knowing Rufus had meant to shoot in the trees right over his head. He never thought the man would really take a gun after them.

At least the shotgun was pointed skyward. Hopefully Rufus was just blowing off steam, and not foolish enough to go directly against all the McKinnon guns.

Steve used his free hand to push his hat up his forehead and wipe his brow. He sighed, heavy and deep, irritated.

"Like I told you before, Rufus, we ain't touched none of your sheep. Now why don't you get on home? They'll probably be waiting for you."

Rufus circled the barrel of the shotgun in the air. "You've got my sheep hid somewhere, along with them kids and my dog. If'n you don't tell me where they are, you'll have a heap more trouble than you bargained for with them horses."

Steve dropped his hand, looking directly at Rufus. "I had a hunch that rockslide was no act of nature. But you listen to me, mister. You get near my herd or my men again, and it'll be the last thing you do."

Steve shoved his six-gun in his holster and motioned for Stubby and Rebekah to get on the wagon. He shouted at the wranglers, "I said, let's roll them out of here! We're burning daylight."

Jimmy nudged his mare to the corral, undid the leather latch, and turned it loose with a whoop. The other boys joined in and soon they had the herd at a quick trot on the trail out of the Medicine Bow Mountains.

Jimmy glanced back to see Rufus still standing there, shotgun in hand. It looked like he was aiming their way.

But Steve had handled the situation good. The herd and chuckwagon rolled out without another shot.

CHAPTER 13

The ointment Miss Rebekah used on Jimmy for his shoulders helped, but he didn't figure he'd get a lick of sleep in that first camp they made after leaving the mountain camp.

He gingerly pulled his shirt over his bare shoulders with a wince. Miss Rebekah capped the bottle of ointment and lightly rubbed her knuckles in his shaggy hair.

"You'll make it, Just Jimmy. You're one tough hombre."

Jimmy answered with a moan. He was seated on a stump where Stubby had built the campfire, put on coffee, and was unloading pots from the chuckwagon to start supper.

Lucky Saunders bent over the fire with his own groan, his eyes barely open. He poured himself a cup of the tepid coffee, took a sip, then spit it into the fire.

"You can take your socks out of the coffee pot, Stubs, they should be clean now."

Stubby looked ready to cuss, but he glanced at Rebekah and went back to detangling his pots from the canvas tents in the chuckwagon. Supper was going to be late. Everything was late, and everyone was in a sour mood. The chuckwagon had fallen behind the main group with the two injured men who rode slower.

There were times when the herd nearly got away from the wranglers, galloping down their own trails through the mountain. It was all the wranglers could do to keep the herd together and then tucked into the rope corral at dark.

With the extra work of setting up a rope corral, Jimmy didn't know how Steve's plan was going to work. But the most important thing was to get the horses to Drybone. They could let Laramie decide what to do then. Steve seemed burned out with all the big decisions he had to make.

Maybe that was why he was so snappy. He came into the circle of campfire light and tore into Jimmy.

"I thought I told you to stay out with the herd first watch, not come here and get babied by Doc Beck. You raised by your mother or something?"

Miss Rebekah spoke up. "Steve, Jimmy will need to eat his supper."

Jimmy slowly stood, slipping one suspender over his hot shoulder. He was so sore, he could hardly move. "I'm heading to the corral right now, Steve."

"You should've already been there."

Jimmy drew his other arm through his suspenders. Lucky Saunders handed him a cup of lukewarm coffee. "You've been pushing us awful hard, Steve," Lucky said, his tone tart. "You ought to leave the boy alone."

Steve rounded on him. "You the new boss here?"

"What in blue blazes is this!"

The shout came from the back of the chuckwagon as Stubby yanked out the last canvas tent and threw it to the ground. He planted his fists on his hips, staring into the wagon.

Jimmy shuffled behind with Lucky, Steve, and Rebekah to join Stubby. He peered around them to see three dirt-smeared faces illuminated by the lantern Stubby had hung on the back of the wagon. A furry black-and-white face popped up next to the Palmer triplets.

Stubby barked, "All right, you four tramps, out of my wagon."

Miss Rebekah lifted Roy to the ground as Wayne and Willie scrambled off. Valor the dog leapt down, her tail wagging.

Steve scowled. "As if we didn't have enough trouble with that Rufus."

Rebekah stroked the top of Roy's head as he clung to her. "We'll have to see them back to their cabin."

Willie shrank against the tailgate of the chuckwagon while Wayne reached deep into the man-sized jacket he wore. "You ain't got to take us back! We got these to pay our way."

From his pockets, he produced a tobacco pouch and a gold watch. He held it up by the chain, letting it dangle and catch light from the fire.

Steve frowned and looked at Jimmy as though he were solely responsible for this new headache.

Jimmy beckoned to Wayne and the boy handed over the loot. "I reckon these belong to your uncle, don't they? We'll have to return them or else it's stealing. And that ain't right. You know that, don't ya?"

Jimmy wondered if these kids had anyone who taught them right from wrong. He reckoned he was as good a person as any to teach them. He learned this lesson early in life from a boy who got in trouble for stealing and laid the blame on Jimmy.

He never wanted to suffer that kind of punishment again, along with the shame of feeling he'd done something so wrong.

Jimmy stuffed the tobacco pouch and gold watch in his pocket before squatting down to the kids' level. "Miss Rebekah is pert-near always right and she is this time. You fellows—and girl—can't go with us. I'm sorry."

A tear rolled down Willie's face but she brushed it away along with her stringy hair hanging over her eyes.

"Ain't no reason for us to go back. The sheep herd is gone and Uncle Rufus don't want us. We got nowhere to go."

Sharp pain stabbed Jimmy's heart. He knew how these kids felt, but still looked to Miss Rebekah.

She smiled gently at the children. "Be that as it may, we have to straighten things out with your uncle. I'll see you get there safely myself."

She glanced at Steve, as if letting him know she wasn't going to take time away from his bronc busters. Yet they all knew good and well she couldn't go alone.

Steve dragged his hand over his face with an agitated sigh. "I can't spare a man to send back with you." He dropped his hand and glared at Jimmy. "Guess I can spare a boy, though."

Supper was quiet even as Miss Rebekah spoke with the children. They didn't say much, yet ate plenty. Jimmy liked seeing that, but he hated seeing them go back to Rufus. That man couldn't take care of himself, let alone the kids.

Jimmy ate slowly, at Miss Rebekah's insistence, and nearly fell asleep leaned against a log near the fire. He was jolted by Lucky Saunders, who leaned low and said, "I'll take first watch, Jimmy. Don't mind Steve, he's just feeling his oats."

Jimmy could only nod his appreciation. Lucky started to stand, then bent close.

"Just 'cause Miss Becka asked Steve to be nice to you don't make you no less one of us. She feels a might sorry for you, is all, but you're coming along fine."

CHAPTER 14

The campfire Jimmy built for Miss Rebekah and the triplets the next night wasn't much different than the McKinnon camp where the boys would still be after working horses all day. This campfire burned bright and hot, the flames sparking into the night sky.

Yet everything seemed different to Jimmy as he poked at the burning wood, stirring the fire. Miss Rebekah scooped up plates of beans and hard tack for the kids as they sat like three turtles on a log.

They weren't far from Rufus' cabin, but when they arrived that afternoon, they found it empty and no sign of Rufus. They spent the rest of the daylight hours searching for him and for any sign of the missing sheep.

The only thing Jimmy detected was the sheep herd being driven from the meadow, hoof prints of three saddled horses trailing the sheep. He lost the trail in the loose rocks.

Jimmy thought again of the men he'd seen camped in the valley, and wished he'd followed through with keeping a close eye on them. But his first duty was to his work for Doctor McKinnon. He sure wasn't doing that tonight as he sat by the campfire with the triplets and Miss Rebekah.

She had concluded there was nothing they could do but take the kids with them and hope to find their uncle in Drybone.

But that wasn't what was bothering Jimmy. What Lucky Saunders told him last night was tearing up Jimmy inside.

He accepted a plate of beans from Miss Rebekah, eyes downcast. She held onto the plate until he looked up at her, concern in her eyes. That made it all worse.

Jimmy shook his head and she released the plate. He wasn't hankering to talk.

The three kids downed their beans, then set their plates on the ground for Valor to lap the juice after her own plate of beans.

Rebekah sat with her hands folded on her knees as she talked with the kids, then spent time working with Roy, showing him how to use his hands to talk. She had told Jimmy she hoped they could find an orphanage for the kids where they could teach Roy sign language, if they couldn't find a family that would take the three in.

Jimmy bit his tongue against asking if they could be that family, on account of he and Miss Rebekah weren't really a family.

"Mr. Jimmy, how come you keep looking down like that?"

The question came from Willie as she scooted closer to the fire on the chilly mountain evening.

Jimmy glanced up, realizing they all watched him. He shifted to set his half-eaten plate of beans in front of the dog. She lapped it up as she continued laying at the feet of Wayne, seated on the log.

Jimmy tried to muster something carefree to say. "Why, every cowpoke on the range knows you ain't supposed to stare into a fire at night. Some wolf or a rustler comes up on the camp and you won't be able to see them because the light of the fire will still be in your eyes."

The kids nodded solemnly as though he just imparted some great notion. Jimmy didn't feel too smart.

He rubbed his hands on his trousers. "You kids best turn in. Y'all need to get some sleep so we can catch up with the crew tomorrow."

The kids didn't argue. They were relieved they hadn't found their uncle, and were going ahead with the ranch hands like they planned.

It wasn't long before they were snoozing, Valor curled on top of Roy who slept between his brother and sister.

Once the first earnest snore sounded, Miss Rebekah scooted over to take a seat next to Jimmy. She folded her hands on her knees again.

"All right, young man, out with it. What's bothering you?"

Jimmy stared at the ground. "I don't rightly know, Miss Rebekah. I reckon I keep thinking about those kids and their uncle. He... he makes me think of my pa."

There was a long stretch of silence, broken only by the fire popping. Miss Rebekah finally asked, "Where is your father now, Jimmy?"

He rubbed a hand over his mouth, feeling the calluses on his palms from years of hard ranch work. He'd been doing it since he ran away from that last orphanage where they took the rod serious whether you did anything wrong or were just accused of it. Like stealing.

His rough thumb caught something wet on his face. A tear.

Jimmy scrubbed it away and cleared his throat. "I never met my pa. Just heard tell about him. They put him in prison when I was a baby, locked him up for beating on a woman."

"A woman?"

"My ma. They said she died from it."

Miss Rebekah let out a little gasp and put her arm around Jimmy's shoulders.

He quickly stood, shoving his hands into his pocket, feeling the gold watch in one and the tobacco pouch in the other. He would have left both in Rufus' cabin, but it looked like the man might have cleared out.

Jimmy rushed to say, "You ain't got to feel sorry for me, Miss Rebekah. The Good Lord's always taken care of me, and I reckon He'll keep on even when I'm on my own again."

Rebekah stood, the confusion on her face illuminated by the fire. "I've never felt sorry for you, Jimmy. I'm quite proud of you."

Jimmy shifted his jaw, staring over the top of the fire. "Then why did you ask Steve to look after me, like I'm some tenderfoot that needs a nursemaid?"

Miss Rebekah reached out and tipped Jimmy's jaw, getting him to meet her eyes. There was nothing but pure truth in hers.

"That's not what happened, Jimmy. At least, not entirely. It wasn't really for you, it was for Steve. You see, I helped him get on his feet when he first came west and I'm proud of how he's become head wrangler on the ranch. I don't want his jealousy of you and Laramie Jones to ruin that."

Jimmy scrunched his eyebrows together. "What do you mean, jealous of me?"

Rebekah sighed. "Laramie took Steve under his wing and taught him everything he knew. Laramie is doing the same with you, and I suppose Steve felt he was losing his special place. But something he needs to learn is that Laramie's heart is big enough for all you boys."

Jimmy blew out a big breath, the sick feeling leaving his stomach. Maybe he'd get another plate of beans. "I'm awful glad to hear that, Miss Rebekah...I mean, about you not feeling sorry for me."

She patted his shoulder and sighed heavy. "That doesn't mean I'm not sorry for the things you've been through, especially because of your father. Have you ever..."

Miss Rebekah didn't finish.

Valor let out a low *woof*, causing Jimmy to turn and see where she had lifted her head. She was looking into the darkness beyond the fire. Kate was restless too, tossing her head from where she and the other horses were hobbled.

Jimmy pulled his hands out of his pockets, but not in time.

Coming barely into the light of the camp were three armed men on horseback.

CHAPTER 15

O ne rifle and one shotgun were pointed at Jimmy while the third man had his six-gun out. Arm crossed over his saddle horn, he let the pistol dangle relaxed but ready.

Jimmy was still wearing his six-gun, but it didn't do much good in the holster.

The kids were coming awake. Valor got up on her four paws, balanced on Roy's back. She barked at the intruders.

The armed men chuckled. "Well now, it was sure accommodating of you folks to bring that dog back. Those dumb sheep don't know nothing about being herded by horses."

One of the men threw a coiled lariat rope over the fire. It landed by the kids.

"One of you tie her up and bring her over here."

The triplets were sitting up now, wide-eyed. Roy wrapped his arms around Valor's neck and Jimmy knew there was no way he was going to let go. These men didn't look like they had any patience for a mute boy.

Jimmy took a step toward the fire, catching the men's attention as they stiffened. He spread his hands to show he wasn't making a play for his gun.

"I don't reckon she'll do you boys much good," he said, slow and easy. "Don't you know what kind of dog that is?"

The men furrowed their brows, confused. Jimmy, keeping his right hand out and away from his gun, used his left to reach into his pocket. He retrieved the tobacco pouch as he kept talking.

"This here is a collie, a special herding breed, and she's one of the best I've ever seen. But there's something real peculiar about this kind of dog."

Jimmy opened the pouch, keeping his movements steady. He got one of the paper squares and tapped tobacco into it the way he'd seen cowhands do it a thousand times.

"These dogs are born loyal to one master. If that master dies before the dog, why, she just lays on her master's grave and dies, too." He pulled the drawstring closed with his teeth and tucked the pouch in his jacket pocket. "Can't nobody get her to do anything else."

Jimmy rolled the smoke and licked the wrap to seal it. He was aware of Miss Rebekah standing just slightly behind him, and could feel her tension. Jimmy didn't smoke.

The men, intrigued by his storytelling, sat unmoving on their horses. Then the man with the pistol scoffed. "She'll learn to take to her new master, or she'll find herself in a grave instead of laying on one."

Jimmy squatted and picked up a twig near the fire. He lit one end of the twig and straightened, still holding the smoke.

"You can shoot her, but that would be a powerful waste."

"Maybe so, but those sheep don't do us no good if they keep scattering over the mountainside." The man pointed his pistol at the kids. "You there, the littlest one, you tie up that dog and bring her here. Kiss your brother and sister goodbye, too, because you're coming with us—just to make sure this smart aleck cowpoke don't follow."

Jimmy swallowed, hard. He'd let the dog go before he endangered the kids or Miss Rebekah. But if those men took little Roy, they'd never see the boy alive again.

The twig was burned halfway down now. Jimmy held it close to his body. "Like I said, she won't take to a new master, and that little boy don't know how to tell her what to do."

The man with the double-barreled shotgun cocked both hammers.

"Maybe we'll just put your theory to the test about mourning her master." He was looking at Wayne and Willie.

The twig burned down to Jimmy's fingertips. It was time. He calculated the three men, their positions, and the position of their guns.

Then Miss Rebekah did what he hoped she would. As the twig's flame touched his bare skin, she screamed, "Jimmy, look out!"

Jimmy yelped and flung the burning twig to the ground. In one continuous motion, he brought his hand up again, gripping the butt of his six-gun. It was out and spitting fire in half a blink.

The first bullet struck the man with the shotgun, hitting him in the shoulder and causing his hand to jerk on the trigger.

Both barrels cut loose, hitting his partner beside him, and made the pistol man's horse rear. The man with the shotgun tumbled to the ground along with his partner. But the pistol man was bringing his gun over his horse's neck and taking aim at Jimmy.

Jimmy fanned the hammer on his six-gun, double firing. The bullets struck the pistol man in the gun arm, and again in the other arm. The man dropped over his horse's neck, gasping. The horse danced in a circle.

"Hold it right there, all of you!" A familiar voice shouted.

Steve, Lucky Saunders, and two other McKinnon hands galloped into the camp, guns trained on the three wounded men. Lucky sprang from his saddle and rounded up the rustlers' guns.

Steve swung his horse and his attention to the camp—namely Jimmy.

Smoking six-gun aimed at the ground, Jimmy was frozen in a half crouch.

Miss Rebekah shook his arm. "Breathe, Jimmy. Breathe."

Jimmy sucked in an enormous breath, tasting metallic gun powder.

He coughed. Doubling over, he dashed for the log he sat on earlier to eat his supper, and promptly lost it on the other side of the log.

From beside him, Wayne whistled. "I ain't never going to stare into a fire ever again."

Rebekah rubbed the back of Jimmy's neck and offered him a handkerchief. Her voice trembled as she said, "I've never seen anything quite like that."

From behind Jimmy, Steve echoed, "Me neither. Best shooting of any man I've ever known. That, or the Good Lord's sure looking out for him."

CHAPTER 16

The starched collar of his new shirt scratched Jimmy's neck. It felt like a hangman's noose, but with how Steve and Laramie were trussed up for the evening, Jimmy could do no less. Besides, it was a dark red one made by Miss Rebekah herself, and when she gave it to Jimmy, he felt like there was a special reason behind it. Like it was a going away present, even though she hadn't left.

They might not always be together, but the shirt would keep her right over his heart.

Every seat at the formal dining room table in Doctor McKinnon's home was occupied at this celebration dinner. Somehow, the McKinnon wranglers, led by Steve, had successfully fulfilled the horse contract, delivering the combined herds to Fort McKinney. Laramie Jones had pulled back before they arrived at the fort and let Steve take care of the business. Steve was nervous, but Jimmy watched him negotiate a contract for next year—one with reasonable expectations this time.

Jimmy was elbow to elbow with Steve, who sat on one side of Laramie with Miss Rebekah on Laramie's other side. Jimmy normally sat next to her, but this arrangement felt right.

Miss Rebekah, Mr. Laramie, Steve, and him. It felt like family.

Wayne, Willie, and Roy were seated between Miss Rebekah and Doc McKinnon. With part of his bonus for the long drive, Jimmy promised to buy circus tickets for all three of the kids.

They were reserved in the "palace" as they called the house, but seemed awfully happy about the older couple across the table from them. Since the crew found Rufus and his sheep, the man said he had no use for the kids and it wasn't hard to convince him to allow the triplets to go on with the wranglers all the way back to McKinnon Ranch, and then their new home.

The couple at the table weren't able to have children of their own, and were welcoming the "blackberry cobbler kids" into their lives. Another cause to celebrate.

Rebekah had asked Jimmy why he started calling the Palmer triplets the "blackberry cobbler kids." He said it was because they were sweet, but kind of messy.

She laughed and Jimmy was awful glad she was still his best friend. He wanted to go with her wherever she went, but if God ever split their trails, it would be all right. They'd always be together in spirit.

Brendan Peele and his daughter Daphne were among those who occupied places at the table, celebrating the future contract that Mr. Peele was already committing to be part of.

Brendon Peele, his walrus mustache twitching, looked sideways down the table at Jimmy. "I heard from Steve that if it wasn't for you, the operation in the Medicine Bow Mountains would've been a bust. I know McKinnon prides himself on having the best hands, but I'm keeping an eye on you myself."

From beneath a cluster of curled bangs, Daphne Peele batted her eyelashes at Jimmy.

He gulped.

Steve elbowed him and whispered, "Looks like you're getting married or buried, Jimmy."

He squeezed his eyes shut like he did when he was on the

back of a bronc, the moment feeling as jarring as slamming down in the saddle.

Steve's teasing words tickled his ear when he said, "Don't you worry, Just Jimmy. I'll be with you every step of the way...right down the aisle."

And Jimmy knew he truly had a home for good on the McKinnon Ranch, with the Good Lord and friends looking out for him.

Dearest reader,

Thank you for reading *Bronc Buster (Doc Beck Westerns Book 6)*. I truly hope it entertained and delighted you!

If you fell in love with the main characters, Rebekah, aka "Doc Beck," and Jimmy, you'll be excited to know book 7, *The Gunman*, is available! You can order it on any major retail site or through www.SarahElisabethWrites.com.

I'd be thrilled if you took a moment to write your thoughts in the form of a review for *Bronc Buster* and post it on your favorite retail outlet and Goodreads. You'll help other readers find this series.

To discover more of my books, free short stories, and to generally stay in touch with me, I invite you to join my VIP reader newsletter. You'll receive a free copy of *The Executions*, book one in my historical fiction *Choctaw Tribune* Series. Please join me through: bit.ly/ChoctawTribune.

Speaking of history, the character of Doc Beck was inspired by Dr. Susan La Flesche (Omaha), who is hailed as the first American Indian to earn a medical degree. In continued research, my mother found Dr. Isabel Cobb (Cherokee), the first woman physician in Indian Territory, in very nearly the same years as Dr. La Flesche.

Lastly, if you're not familiar with my heritage books based on my Choctaw history and culture, you can check them out on www.SarahElisabethWrites.com.

Questions? Send them my way: me@sarahelisabethwrites.com

—Sarah Elisabeth Sawyer
Historical Fiction and Western author
Tribal member of the Choctaw Nation of Oklahoma

CANYON WAR (DOC BECK WESTERNS BOOK 1)

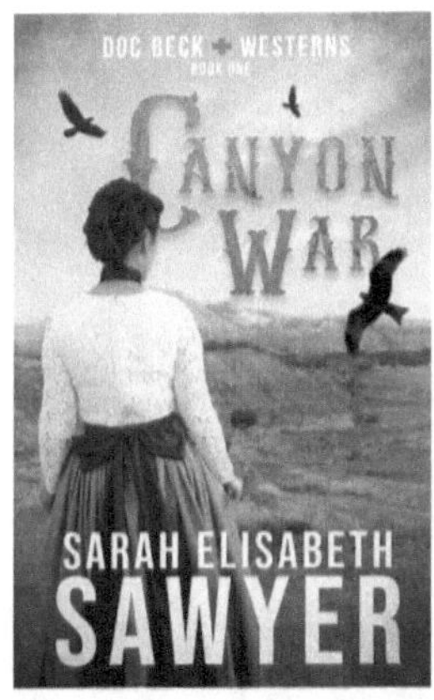

Traveling the West as a female physician, 34-year-old Doctor Rebekah LaRoche is no stranger to trouble. But on her way to New Mexico Territory, an unexpected stay in Amarillo, Texas, leads to confrontation with the Baxter clan – four brothers bred for trouble – and finds Rebekah in deep trouble.

Cattle rancher Clem Baxter's private war over grazing rights in the Palo Duro Canyon turns disastrous, and when the dust settles, one of the Baxter brothers is hurt bad. Clem sends for a doctor, not a woman, but that's what he gets when Rebekah, known as "Doc Beck," arrives at the ranch.

Now held at Clem's ranch against her will, Rebekah must plot to flee through the night with her young friend into the dangers and beauty of the Palo Duro Canyon.

Of Omaha Indian and French descent, Rebekah has always relied on her wits to get her out of any situation. But does that include facing down men willing to die—and kill—for a wild piece of land just as dangerous as any bullet?

***Canyon War* is available on multiple retailer sites.**

♦ ♦ ♦

MISSION BANDITS (DOC BECK WESTERNS BOOK 2)

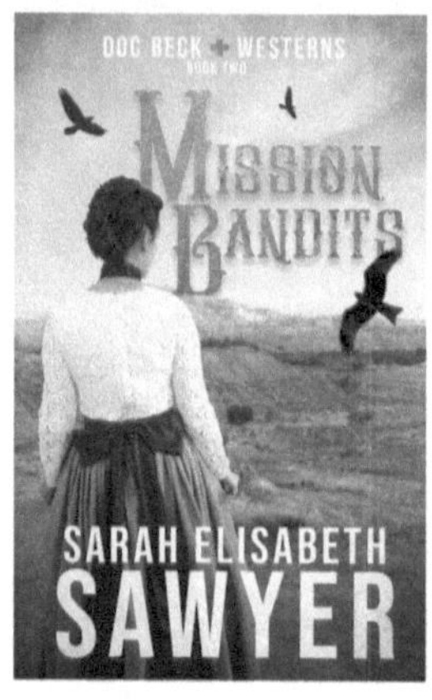

The Mexican army, a town marshal, and the Sancho Guerra gang are facing off when Doctor Rebekah LaRoche and her new friend, Jimmy, arrive in Zapata, New Mexico Territory. The bandits are holding hostages at Hope Academy, a school for girls located in an old mission outside of town, and Rebekah feels compelled to act—she was sent to the school to modernize the infirmary, not see the innocent occupants murdered.

The notorious and charismatic bandit, Sancho Guerra, led his band of men on a pillaging spree from Mexico to the mission and has proven his indifference to killing, prepared for any tricks the army or the Zapata town marshal throw at him.

But he isn't prepared for Rebekah, and now the Mexican army colonel wants her to do something terrifying—enter the mission and help with the capture of the deadliest men in the territory.

***Mission Bandits* is available on multiple retailer sites.**

◆◆◆

❖ ❖ ❖

DESERT CAPTIVE (DOC BECK WESTERNS BOOK 4)

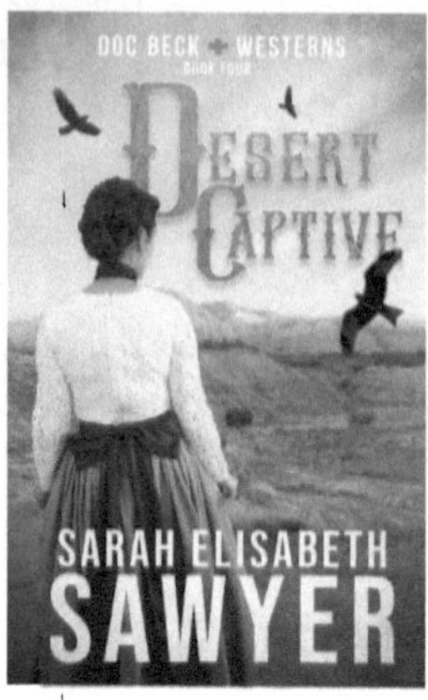

If thou knewest the gift of God...thou wouldest have asked of him, and he would have given thee living water...

There comes a time when one questions every decision they've made in life. That moment is here for Doctor Rebekah LaRoche when she is taken captive by her nemesis, the bandit Sancho Guerra, and spirited across the desert to a hidden village in Mexico.

With no hope of rescue, Rebekah must earn a place among the families of bandits as a medical doctor until she can devise a way to reach the top of the road leading out of the valley—without being shot by the three sets of guards.

Little does Rebekah know that her long-time friend, Laramie Jones, is on his way to attempt a hopeless rescue. If she knew his plans, she'd beg him to stay away: no one has ever penetrated the bandits' valley and lived to tell about it.

With factions closing in all around her, time is ticking down toward an explosive conclusion, and Rebekah will have to draw on her greatest strength yet to survive.

Desert Captive is available on multiple retailer sites.

♦♦♦

RANCH FEUD (DOC BECK WESTERNS BOOK 5)

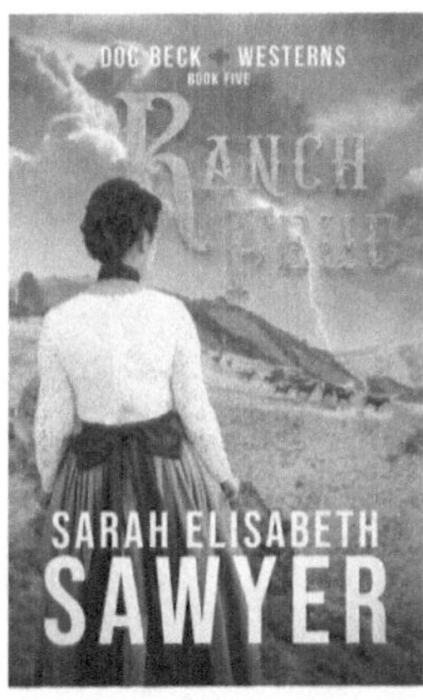

A feud dating back to the Civil War threatens Doc Beck's future...

Doctor Rebekah LaRoche is finally home in Wyoming—but trouble waits for her in spades, and a slim chance to return to the Omaha Indian Reservation grows slimmer when she's drawn into a feud between two powerful ranchers.

Glenn Butler and Dean Wallace hate each other's guts and have pitted their offspring against each other since birth. But it's Butler's daughter, Lilly, and her disgrace at law school that has Rebekah scrambling for answers. Rebekah wrote the letter of recommendation that helped Lilly be accepted into the college, and if she can't untangle the scandal and its connection to this powerful rivalry, she is doomed with another black mark on her professional reputation.

U.S. Senator Jeffrey Harris wants Rebekah to stay out of the young state's troubles if she hopes to have his help. But how can she stay out of something that's entangled her, threatening the last chance she has to return to her people?

Ranch Feud **is available on multiple retailer sites.**

♦ ♦ ♦

THE GUNMAN (DOC BECK WESTERNS BOOK 7)

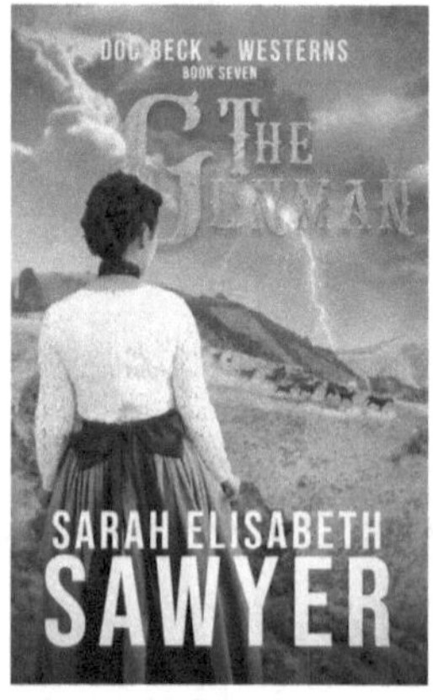

"Whatever you do, stay out of trouble."

The echo of Doctor McKinnon's words follow Doctor Rebekah LaRoche on her latest medical mission. But being tasked with escorting an unknown woman to an insane asylum is difficult enough; add in former gunman Cord Johnson, who claims to be the woman's brother, and Rebekah is set on a dangerous path to discover the truth about the silent woman before it's too late.

Cord Johnson's violent reputation haunts him on his quest to keep a promise made to his sister—a promise he is determined to keep after breaking so many. All he wants to do is to take Ella home to the farm their father left them and live in peace. But when a rogue U.S. marshal arrests him for murder and Doctor Rebekah LaRoche takes off with his sister, Cord must rely on the reputation of his ivory handled six-guns.

With an upcoming political meeting to state her case for returning home to the Omaha Indian Reservation, the last thing Rebekah needs is to get tangled up with a gunman and a lost woman who is unable to speak for herself. But could Cord Johnson be telling the truth? Is Rebekah set to commit the emotionally distraught woman to an asylum that will separate a family forever?

***The Gunman* is available on multiple retail sites.**

APE MAN (DOC BECK WESTERNS BOOK 8)

"He's dead."

When Doctor Rebekah LaRoche makes the pronouncement in Senator Jeffrey Harris' office, her world is rocked by the death—and the note found beside the deceased. It's addressed to her personally: an ominous warning that those in her life always end up worse off because of her.

While the Donavan Brothers Circus rolls into Centennial Ridge, Wyoming, a murderous stalker tracks Rebekah's every move and targets those she loves. Death and near-death follow her in a terrifying sequence. But when Just Jimmy finds himself in the stalker's crosshairs, Rebekah unravels, ready to give up her quest to return home to the Omaha Indian Reservation for fear of endangering her relatives there.

Nowhere is truly safe for Rebekah as long as deadly secrets stalk her and tests of faith, regret, and forgiveness culminate in the Medicine Bow Mountains as a single terrifying fight for her own survival. "Doc Beck" has saved many lives—but can she save her own?

***Ape Man* is available on multiple retail sites.**

◆ ◆ ◆

THE EXECUTIONS (CHOCTAW TRIBUNE SERIES, BOOK 1)

Who would show up for their own execution?

It's 1892, Indian Territory. A war is brewing in the Choctaw Nation as two political parties fight out issues of old and new ways. Caught in the middle is eighteen-year-old Ruth Ann, a Choctaw who doesn't want to see her family killed.

In a small but booming pre-statehood town, her mixed blood family owns a controversial newspaper, the *Choctaw Tribune*. Ruth Ann wants to help spread the word about critical issues but there is danger for a female reporter on all fronts—socially, politically, even physically.

But what is truly worth dying for? This quest leads Ruth Ann and her brother Matthew, the stubborn editor of the fledgling *Choctaw Tribune*, to old Choctaw ways at the farm of a condemned murderer. It also brings them to head on clashes with leading townsmen who want their reports silenced no matter what.

More killings are ahead. Who will survive to know the truth? Will truth survive?

The Executions **is available on multiple retailer sites.**

◆ ◆ ◆

TRAITORS (CHOCTAW TRIBUNE SERIES, BOOK 2)

"Someone's going to be king in this territory.

No reason it can't be me. It sure won't be you."

Betrayed.

Someone is tearing at the fabric of the Choctaw Nation while political turmoil, assassinations, and feuds threaten the very sovereignty of the tribe. It stands under the U.S. government's scrutiny.

When heated words turn to hot lead, Ruth Ann Teller—a mixed-blood Choctaw—fears losing her brother who won't settle for anything but the truth. Matthew is determined to use his newspaper, the *Choctaw Tribune*, to uncover the scheme behind Mayor Thaddeus Warren's claim to the townsite of Dickens. Matthew is willing to risk his newspaper—and his life—to uncover a traitor among their Choctaw people.

But when Ruth Ann tries to help, she causes more harm than good—especially after the mayor brings in Lance Fuller, a schoolteacher from New York. How does this charming yet aloof young man fit into the mayor's scheme?

When attacks against the newspaper strike and bullets fly, a trip to the Chicago World's Fair of 1893 is the answer they need to save the Choctaw Tribune. The trip holds a key to Matthew's investigation.

But Ruth Ann must find the courage to face a journey to the White City —without her brother.

***Traitors* is available on multiple retailer sites.**

♦ ♦ ♦

SHAFT OF TRUTH (CHOCTAW TRIBUNE SERIES, BOOK 3)

"Nothing to it but a stout heart."

On a mission to bring justice to the outlaw gang that murdered his father and brother, Matthew Teller leaves the *Choctaw Tribune* newspaper for his sister to operate and plunges into an unfamiliar world of darkness and danger. Working inside the coal mines of the Choctaw Nation—one of the most dangerous places in the country—he searches for a man who may have the answers to this six-year-old mystery. But after Matthew uncovers an earth-shattering truth that rocks him to his core, he must decide what right is, and what price he is willing to pay for it.

Ruth Ann Teller knows she can handle publishing the *Choctaw Tribune*—until she loses their biggest advertiser. Now, with Matthew miles away and the future of the newspaper resting squarely on her shoulders, Ruth Ann must make a bold move to keep the newspaper afloat in her brother's absence. She sets it on a course for new success or total disaster.

Striking coal miners. Outlaw gangs. An unsolved crime. And a Choctaw family that fights for one another, and for truth.

Shaft of Truth (_Choctaw Tribune_ Series, Book 3) is available on multiple retailer sites.

◆ ◆ ◆

ANUMPA WARRIOR: CHOCTAW CODE TALKERS OF WORLD WAR I

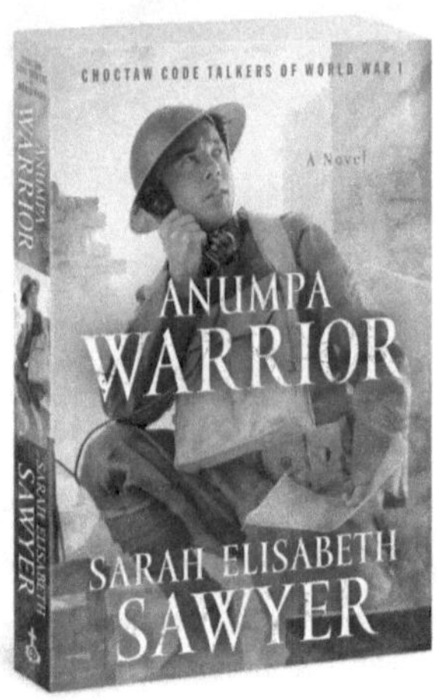

The day I betrayed Isaac, I vowed never again to speak my native language in front of white men.

When America enters the Great War in 1917, Bertram Robert Dunn and his Choctaw buddies from Armstrong Academy join the army to protect their homes, their families, and their country. Hoping to find redemption for a horrible lie that betrayed his best friend, B.B. heads into the trenches of France—but what he discovers is a duty only his native tongue can fulfill.

War correspondent Matthew Teller is ready to quit until an encounter with a fellow Choctaw sets him on a path to write the untold story of

American Indian doughboys. But entrenched stereotypes and prejudices tear at his burning desire to spread truth.

With the Allies building toward the greatest offensive drive of the war, the American Expeditionary Forces face a superior enemy who intercepts their messages and knows their every move. Can the solution come from a people their own government stripped of culture and language?

Anumpa Warrior **is available on multiple retailer sites.**

TOUCH MY TEARS: TALES FROM THE TRAIL OF TEARS

For this collection of short stories, Choctaw authors from five U.S. states came together to present a part of their ancestors' journey, a way to honor those who walked the trail for their future. These stories not only capture a history and a culture, but the spirit, faith, and resilience of the Choctaw people.

Tears of sadness. Tears of joy. Touch and experience them.

Touch My Tears **is available on multiple retailer sites.**

◆ ◆ ◆

TUSHPA'S STORY (Touch My Tears Collection)

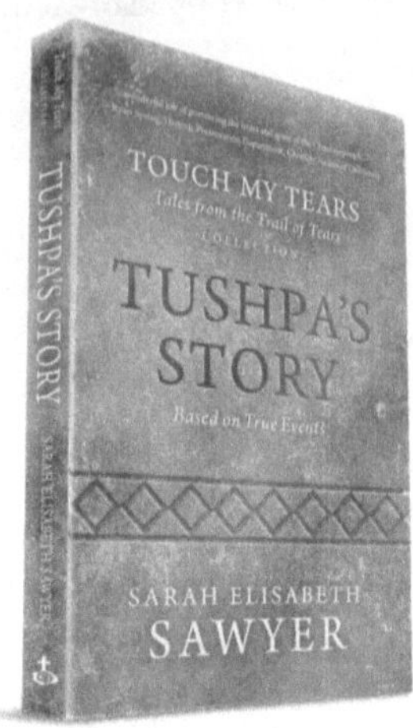

"Protect the book as you do our seed corn. We must have both to survive."

The Treaty of Dancing Rabbit Creek changed everything. The Choctaw Nation could no longer remain in their ancient homelands.

Young Tushpa, his family, and their small band embark on a trail of life and death. More death than life lay ahead.

On their journey to a new homeland, the faith of his father and one book guide Tushpa as he learns what it means to become a man and a leader.

But before long, betrayal from within and without rip at the unity of the band. Can Tushpa help keep his tattered people together? Or will they all be lost to sickness of the mind, body, and spirit on the four hundred mile walk?

A continuation of the anthology *Touch My Tears: Tales from the Trail of Tears*, this story follows an original manuscript written by Tushpa's son, James Culberson.

Tushpa's Story is available on multiple retailer sites.

SARAH ELISABETH SAWYER is a story archaeologist. She digs up shards of past lives, hopes, and truths, and pieces them together for readers today. The Smithsonian's National Museum of the American Indian honored her as a literary artist through their Artist Leadership Program for her work in preserving Choctaw Trail of Tears stories. A tribal member of the Choctaw Nation of Oklahoma, she writes historical fiction from her hometown in Texas, partnering with her mother, Lynda Kay Sawyer, in continued research for future works. Learn more at SarahElisabethWrites.com, Facebook.com/SarahElisabethSawyer

www.ingramcontent.com/pod-product-compliance
Lightning Source LLC
Chambersburg PA
CBHW030647190726
48286CB00008B/2695